EXIT WOUND

By Alexandra Moore

Exit Wound

Limitless Publishing, LLC
Kailua, HI 96734
www.limitlesspublishing.com

Formatting: Limitless Publishing

ISBN-13: 978-1-68058-393-9
ISBN-10: 1-68058-393-X

Dedication

For my two dads: The first, who gave me life and loved me the best way he could, and for the second, who chose me and has never left my side since.
I love you both.

CHAPTER ONE

Even though I had vowed to never be like my mother, there were times I liked to taste sin on the tip of my tongue. Mackynsie made the desire for the taste even worse.

"You ready to go?" she asked. She wasn't drunk at all—though, I was.

"Yeah, sure," I replied. We had just raged on at yet another party. Fall Break was in full swing, and the chilly New York air caused my skin to ripple with little bumps on my arms and chest. I had spilled beer on my jacket, and I didn't really feel like wearing a beer-soaked jacket home. The smell was only bearable for a little bit—although, once I got home, the smell would become something I'd regret.

My apartment always reeked of alcohol and sometimes drugs on a rare occasion, a very rare occasion.

"C'mon, Bea. Time to take you home." Mackynsie didn't sound so pleased about this, but then again, she hadn't been properly pleased since I started going to Rosewood. I knew this was due to the fact that everything had changed in her world and in mine. Mackynsie wanted what I had. I never understood why she did, considering half the time I felt like I had the short end of a shitty stick.

Once I was buckled up and secure in her car, we drove down the long winding road from the countryside and back into the city. I didn't really know the time; all I knew was that it was pitch black outside, which was enough to tell me that I had been out way past my respectable curfew.

Mackynsie turned on the radio, and our favorite song came on: "Heaven Knows" by The Pretty Reckless. We both did our own fangirl montage, singing at the top of our lungs. I was on top of the world, so naturally, I rolled down the window, stuck half of my body out of it, and screamed loudly as we zoomed past a bunch of trees.

"What the hell, Bea! Get yourself back in the car!" Mackynsie tugged on the waistband of my jeans, and as she pulled me in, I felt something. My heart knew before I did. The moment hit me, painfully, etching itself into my mind, and like the artwork I carved into trees, it was permanent. Further down the spiraling road was a driver who was weaving in and out of his lane. Mackynsie was too focused on yelling at me about my reckless actions to notice. I didn't get the chance to say anything to her, because speeding headlights were growing brighter than the sun, and they were heading toward us. A big truck swiped the side of Mackynsie's car, causing the small vehicle to slide across the road, heading toward the trees, spinning us around and around until we crashed into a tree.

After the initial shock of impact, I groaned. I touched my head and the warmth of something liquid surprised me. I knew it was blood.

"M-M-Mackynsie?" I stammered once I found my voice. I heard nothing—though considering the sounds that had been made from the crash and the skidding, I thought that maybe my ears were adjusting to the silence. Only, it couldn't be completely silent. I wasn't alone. I couldn't be alone.

"Mackynsie, are you all right?" I tried to move, but I found that I was too sore to move a muscle. Despite the seatbelt restraining me, I had been tossed around quite a bit.

"Mackynsie?"

I was able to find my phone, and I shined my light against the driver's side of the car. What I saw was unforgettable, and I wanted to be able to forget. I didn't think I could ever forget. Everything I had known was left to die in the mud and rain.

The only difference was that this time I was able to wake up and think of other things. All I could think of was drunk drivers.

I was left alone and angry. Death by car crashes are like lightning bolts within a hurricane. They have the ability to kill everything in its wake and, at the same time, leave the very thing next to it untouched—still breathing and fighting to live.

That was six months ago, and it still felt like it happened yesterday. I was cursed with dreams of my best friend and the car crash that took her life. This dream came to me nearly every night, and other nights, she'd tell me that I should be the one who's dead. It wasn't a dream. It happened to me. I lost my friend. Yet I sat in the dark, repeatedly telling myself, "It's just a dream. Just a bad dream."

This wasn't just a memory or a dream—it was the lightning bolt. I could hear the thunder, yet I never saw it coming, and the only evidence was the exit wound it had left behind.

I pulled my knees up to my chest and wrapped my arms around myself, tucking my head into my arms, trying to recall the soothing breaths that an on-call nurse from the hospital had taught me when I came in that night. I could still remember the saline drip and smell of alcohol on every surface. There was so much blood—I never knew the human body could house so much blood.

I emerged from the crash almost entirely unscathed. I hit my head and sustained a couple of cuts and bruises. That, in conjunction with sore muscles, was meaningless when compared to what had happened to Mackynsie. She was gone before I could even get a last word from her.

We had been best friends since kindergarten, and I couldn't help but feel a new form of emptiness as I went on with the remaining days in school as if she hadn't existed. She was everywhere. Rosewood Academy for the Arts was *her* domain, and I was only the replacement. Rosewood had its own little secret society—The Rosewood Royals—a hierarchy of sorts. The only people who didn't really know about it were the faculty and staff. People left the school wishing they had been the reigning queen of their time at the school. At the time of Mackynsie's death, she had been the reigning Queen Bee.

Crosley was the King, and I was the Queen Regnant. We were days away from graduation, when our ladies and men in waiting would take their places amongst the ranks, replacing us. If I was grateful for anything, it would be the fact that today would be our last day not only as students but as royals. All I wanted was to walk the stage and get the hell out of Dodge. I hadn't told anyone—not even Mackynsie—that I had been accepted into Dartmouth's music college. It would be a big deal because I would be the first in my family to attend college. And this wasn't just any college—this was *Dartmouth*.

I had been waiting to tell my brother Ben, who was the one shelling out the money I needed for application fees and for all the other fees and expenses I had to pay. Since my brother was the breadwinner of the family and everything and since my FAFSA was based on my mother's income—or lack thereof—my brother ended up footing the bill for a lot of my things, even my college fund. Ben had been traveling the world with his band since I was twelve. He and his band, Eden Sank, were pretty popular. I could never go a day without hearing one of their songs or seeing someone wearing one of their t-shirts. I was going to see him and his bandmates at my graduation, and if no one noticed him, maybe everything would be all right. I didn't want my graduation to become a circus ring for my brother's fans. It may be selfish, but I wanted him all to myself that day. I hadn't even ever been able to attend one of his concerts. Everyone else had at least done that.

If I remembered my brother as he was pre-band fame, he wouldn't be one to put out a message across his social media saying:

I'm at Rosewood's grad ceremony!
Row A-3!

Then again, I hadn't seen him in six years, during which I'd grown and changed in ways he couldn't possibly imagine. I could only imagine how much he had changed in his own way.

***

The next morning came all too quickly, and I had a lot to do. My last day at school consisted of paperwork and throwing out old papers from my locker. While most of the students at Rosewood were still in classes for another week, all of us seniors were on cleanup duty. That included me. I was stuck in these dusty halls until every debt was paid and my locker was cleaned out.

"Bea, you headed out to that party tonight?" Crosley asked as he walked across the hall, staring at me devilishly while I tried to decide whether to keep or trash the paper in my hand. I decided to trash it along with old sheets of music and assignments. When Crosley came up to me, I smiled kindly at him. It was what was expected of me.

"Well, Bea? Are you going?" he asked, leaning in close to me. I could smell his breath, and it was horrible.

"Depends, which party?"

He laughed at this and shot me a wink, stalking off with one of his friends. There were so many parties that I wasn't sure how I was going to be able to make an appearance to all of them and be home in time to get enough sleep. The graduation ceremony was tomorrow, and I needed my rest. It took a lot to make me look as hot as I did on any given day. Though I technically wasn't required to attend any of the parties since I wasn't officially Queen of Rosewood, most people expected me to be there anyways. I think they wanted to see if I was as much a party animal without Mackynsie as I was with her.

Rummaging through the last of my locker contents, I found a picture of Mackynsie and me together. We were in eighth grade, and we had gotten back from a carnival on Coney Island. She still had her braces, and they were bright with neon green and pink bands. My hair was frizzier then, and I didn't try to hide the sectoral heterochromia that was in my left eye. It made me remember that I even had it. I wore contacts so often I'd forgotten what my real eyes looked like. Right now, I was wearing violet-colored contacts, and it hid my normal viridian green eyes and the little section of brown that curved underneath my left iris. Ben always loved how unique my eyes were, and I always used to think it was great. However, as I got older, I started to hate it, along with many other parts of me.

"Splint-ass alert!"

Someone was shouting this repeatedly through a megaphone, and when I looked behind me, I saw

Splinter Nightingale. He was a very talented drummer, yet a very unfortunate person amongst the Rosewood Royal Hierarchy, always at the butt end of jokes and teasing. I always tried to convince the boys that teasing him wasn't worth it, but to be honest, calling yourself "Splinter" kind of made it easier to become a target for harassment. Today was our last day, though, and that meant he should be given a break. Plus, I was pretty tired of hearing "Splint-Ass" multiple times a day all week long.

"Frank, leave him alone!" I shouted, slamming my locker door shut. I was above Frank and technically always had been, and as Queen Regnant until midnight tomorrow, I needed to pull rank quickly.

"He's only a commoner, Your Highness," he said.

I rolled my eyes and waved toward Splinter, telling him he could go if he so pleased. He did, and I stopped Frank from following after him.

I held out my hand. "Give me your megaphone." When he handed it over, I stepped up to him, stood near his ear, and spoke into the megaphone loudly.

"We're not in high school anymore. Start acting like it, dickface." I dropped the megaphone into his hand, and he left with his ears ringing.

***

When I got home, I could smell the alcohol reeking from the corners of the apartment.

Mother was home today, and chances were she didn't know who I was. She rarely did. She always called me Brenna. I didn't understand it—it was a part of her sickness. What sickness she had, I couldn't be sure—although, I was certain she was getting worse every day.

I set my backpack on the floor in the entryway and started picking up the trash that was strewn across the living room. It was always a mess in this apartment, no matter how many times I cleaned it. I was picking up what looked like fliers, and I noticed that it was in a trail. Sucking in a deep breath, I rounded the corner, and that's when I screamed at the sight of my brother jumping out at me.

"I'm home!" he shouted. I didn't have time to process what was happening, because soon enough the punch that was meant for the nose of an intruder connected with his nose.

"Damn," he laughed. "You throw a good punch."

***

Even though I'd said I was going to the party, I decided spending time with my brother would be time better spent. Since we had been apart so long, I wanted to get to know him as he was today. We fell asleep around 2AM with Thai food boxes scattered across the living room.

When my phone rang at 6AM, I tried to answer it quietly.

"'Ello?" I whispered in a tired drawl.

"Bea, it's time." I looked at the clocks and saw it was indeed time for the event I had been dreading: The Rosewood Royal Coronation.

"I need to get ready."

"We're outside. Just grab a jacket."

I hung up the phone, grabbed my jacket, and pulled the blanket further over my brother's sleeping body. I left a note telling him I was out running errands, just in case he woke up before I got back. Pulling one boot on each foot as I hobbled outside, I leaped into a large van that held Crosley, the former men and women in waiting, along with all the new initiates. From here, we would go to a top-secret (or so we liked to believe) location that was pretty popular among Rosewood students. From there, we would crown the new King and Queen, and then I would finally be free.

***

The ceremony was uneventful. If Frank hadn't recovered from a possible nosedive into the river, I would have had more fun. I didn't have to do much except put a fake crown on some incoming junior who would be the queen for the next two years unless someone usurped her. I felt sorry for her when I saw her look of pure joy. I prayed that maybe it wouldn't be as bad for her as it was for Mackynsie—or for me. Crosley wasn't necessarily the King of our dreams—then again, is anyone really as they are in our dreams?

When I got home, I gave one last kiss to Crosley, and it left a taste of ashes in my mouth. He was supposed to be my boyfriend, and I never liked kissing him. The touch of his lips against mine felt like a fire that wasn't supposed to be burning. My lips turned to ash against his, and soon enough, I would choke on them.

"See you tonight," he said with a heavy breath, ending the kiss.

"Yeah, hopefully." Without another word, I got out of the van and went back into the apartment where I rushed to get ready. So many hair products and yet so little time to tame my unruly curls.

When I was done, I dressed in a printed maxi skirt and a short white cami, which was probably the girliest thing I owned. I put a big pendant necklace around my neck and went to grab my cap and gown.

"The ceremony is at noon," I said to Ben. "You better be there."

He waved at me from the couch, and I left the apartment, ready to make my way to the subway station. When I got outside, I spotted someone from my not-so-recent-past. Everett Thompson, my brother's drummer.

"Everett?" I said in shock. After an incident when I was sixteen, which still left me with mixed feelings, I hadn't spoken to him much. I missed him. We needed to talk and clarify a few things, but looking at him now with his messy blond hair and his piercing blue eyes, I knew I wanted to be with him more than anything.

"Need a lift?" he asked, leaning against Old Trusty, the car he had left in his older brother's protection while he was gone.

"Yeah, sure," I replied.

He opened the door for me, I got inside, and then he shut the door and went around to the driver's side.

The ride was mainly silent, but when we got to the ceremony site, I wanted nothing more than to feel his lips against mine again, just as I had when I was sixteen. It had only been two years ago—could it be so different?

"Everett—"

"I know, I know. Not today. Let's focus on you today. We'll have plenty of time to catch up." He ran a finger over my cheekbone, and I wondered if my flushed cheeks were growing redder with each caress.

"I should go inside," I said, and he nodded.

"I'll go back and gather the guys when it's time to start," he said. "I'll make sure your brother is ready."

I leaned over and gave him a hug, and with that, I was off to prepare for the rest of my life.

***

The speeches were long, mundane, and cliché. Some were downright unnecessary, and I wondered how the hell the speaker had gotten it approved for the ceremony.

When I walked across the stage and accepted my diploma and shook the hand of the principal, the director and the owner of Rosewood Academy, it was as if a weight I had been carrying inside was pushed aside and thrown away. When I was back at my seat and our school song played, we graduating students flipped the tassels on our caps. My hat went into the air, and I could feel all the weight of high school and the last year and a half fall from my shoulders as my hat cascaded to the ground with the thousands of others right next to it.

I was done with high school. I was free.

I ran to find my brother and spotted him immediately. He was wearing a button down dress shirt with the sleeves rolled up, which showed some of his prominent tattoos. Aviator sunglasses covered his eyes, and his hair was gelled to look perfectly askew. I rushed to hug him, and Everett took a picture of us. Soon enough, people started to take notice of whom I was with. I heard the whispers over the thousands of laughs and conversations taking place. I took one look at my brother and saw he had been crying.

When I made mention of it, he said, "It's allergy season," while he dabbed his eyes with a handkerchief.

"All right, saps. Who's ready for some food?" It was Rian who said this, and he took the sudden increase in attention in stride. It was just like him. Rian was ninety percent ego and ten percent alcohol. Although if you asked him, I believe he would change the variables around a bit. While we were debating about what to get to eat, I saw Rian taking pictures with some girls behind us, and signing their programs while the rest of us did the work.

"I want pizza. LA doesn't have pizza like we do here," Grayson said. Grayson, next to Everett and my brother, was probably one of my favorite people. He was engaged to his high school sweetheart, and they had an eight-year-old daughter together. I still remember when she was born, and how after that Ben was determined to scare me out of ever having sex. Unfortunately, his tactics never worked on me.

"Let's get out of here. I want to spend some time with my favorite sissa," Ben said, wrapping an arm around me. I beamed with pride when he called me his sissa. It was his thing, his really, really odd and silly thing to call me.

Most of the graduating students were on their phones, and others were taking pictures with their friends. I spotted Crosley talking with Frank and a few other guys, and I caught his gaze. I waved goodbye to him. This would be the last time I saw him, and for that I was glad. High school was behind me now, and I wanted to forget about the last four years as quickly as I could. I wanted to start my life somewhere else. In that moment, though, I had to spend time with my brother. High school came and it went, as did the people you met while you were there. With Ben, I knew he would never leave my side now that we were together again. The further we walked away from the crowd of people, the closer he hugged me to him. He missed me just as I had missed him, and I was sure he never wanted to go this long without seeing me again.

***

We ate at a small pizza pub in Times Square, and every five minutes, I was getting notifications on Twitter, Instagram, and Facebook. The embrace between Ben and me had instigated a whole new level of excitement among the graduates as well as the guests. It had been hard to leave once they recognized him along with the rest of the band, and I knew I wouldn't be much of a secret by morning. The whole confidentiality thing was complicated. Ben never hid the fact that he had a sister—though, the subject never came up often, nor did he choose to talk about it candidly. When he did, it was only of how close he was to me, and how he wanted nothing more than the world for me.

When the band was starting to get a lot of hype, he and the record label he was signed under drew up a confidentiality contract. No one was to mention that I was his sister. It wasn't really that difficult to hide. Most people wouldn't guess that I was his sibling, considering how much we differed in appearances. His chestnut hair, coffee bean eyes, and the tone of his light skin differed greatly from my raven-haired, green-eyed and porcelain-don't-even-think-about-tanning skin. I really didn't look like anyone that I've ever known in our family. Then again, I had very little family that was still living to compare myself to. Ben hated not being able to speak openly about me. It wasn't to protect himself, though; it was to protect me and my mother. No one really knew the state of our mother's health, and they didn't know much of me at all. Ben was determined to let me finish school without cameras flashing in my face and people asking me questions about the band 24/7. It was going great until tonight, since everyone now saw that I was the sister he so fondly spoke about on occasion.

The pizza pub wasn't really crowded, and so we were able to eat and talk in peace. Ben said that now everyone had figured out our relation, he was going to have to call his record label's legal sector and talk about a new agreement.

I put my hand on his arm, and smiled at him. "Don't bother." He looked at me with a quizzical glance, and I shrugged. "Everyone is going to know by morning. They'll be asking who I am if they don't already know, and if they don't know, someone is bound to tell them. Ben, I'm eighteen. I think it's time people know who I am."

The boys all agreed with me—though, they didn't want to say anything in front of Ben.

As we all filed into the apartment that night, they told me exactly what they thought in the tiniest of whispers.

When we got home, Mother was gone. Ben didn't worry as much as I did—although, this gave me the grand opportunity to pack for the first leg of his tour he had invited me to accompany him on.

Ben gave me a luggage set as a graduation gift and for the tour. Kind of like a kill-two-birds-with-one-stone gift. It was nice, and it even came with a weekender bag, something I had always wanted when I would spend weekends at Mackynsie's house. Music played in the background as I packed. Ben stood in the doorway to my room, examining it without comment. I wasn't the only thing that had changed since he left; my room had too. Ben would often send me allowances, and I eventually saved enough so I could redo my room. It used to look like a fifth grader lived in it instead of the freshman in high school I had been at the time.

Mackynsie had complained about how silly my room looked and how she had been determined to help me redecorate it. So off we'd gone during the weekend before our first year in high school to buy me a new room. The bed frame was a classic Victorian styled brass rod head and footboard. It was the only thing that stayed in my room after Mackynsie's makeover. The bedding changed from my brother's ratty old quilt to a bohemian styled comforter. It had jewel tones and bright, contrasting patterns and prints. My bed was constantly covered with decorative throw pillows and shabby chic blankets. It was a lot busier than an old, ratty quilt. The walls were no longer bare; they now had bookshelves that reached from the floor to the ceiling, filled with journals, photo books, and novels I had acquired over the years. There was also a small writing desk and an old computer that was about ready to die out on me. I had pictures hung on the walls, some of which I had taken myself, others stock photos I had bought in a store. The paintings I had made myself.

Ben appeared to be thinking really hard, and while I was refolding a t-shirt that seemed a little too ratty to come on the road with me, I tried to think of what questions to ask him. I suppose my silence and his curiosity had led him to go looking through my room, which resulted in him finding the Dartmouth shirt in the corner of my bed.

"What's this?" he asked, picking it up and nearly squealing like a girl when he saw the imprinted name across the front.

"Dartmouth? That's the school you're making me pay for? Damn! Frances, I knew you were near genius status, but wow."

It took me by surprise when he called me Frances. He always did simply because it was my first name. I preferred going by a shortened version of my middle name, Beatrice, hence why everyone called me Bea. Ben always called me Frances, unless I was in trouble or he wanted my attention.

I shook my head and promptly took the shirt from him and packed it away. "Shut up, Ben. It's no big deal."

"'No big deal'? Bea, you're the first in the family to go to college. You're the one who is going to *change* things for this family."

Folding another shirt and fitting it into the suitcase, I looked to my brother in annoyance. "*You* changed things for this family, Ben. I'm changing things for *me*."

He was ready to argue, and in that moment, I wasn't sure if I was ready to argue with him. We had never argued, and yet he was so ready to start a fight with me. Then we heard the sound of something breaking in the distance and Grayson's voice yelling something about alcohol. Everett came in without warning, and I could smell the scent of vodka coming from the living area.

"Rian is on a bender again," he announced, which was enough to send Ben out of the room, completely forgetting about the argument we were about have.

Now Everett and I were alone, and I looked at him with my contact-covered eyes and a cheap lipstick smile.

"You look really pretty tonight," he told me, moving closer with every word.

"Thanks."

Then he was right in front of me, staring into my eyes. That's when he noticed the difference. They were violet instead of their normal green.

"What's wrong with your eyes?"

"Contacts," I admitted.

"Take them out—you don't need them."

I shook my head. "I like them, don't you?"

Everett cupped my face, and his other hand wrapped around my waist. "I like the real you. You don't need violet contacts to be pretty to me."

His lips brushed against mine. It was as if I was in my own little world, and for a moment, I really was. Then I heard the wind chimes. Turning to look toward my window, I saw I had left it open—and that there was a dark, hooded figure ready to flee. I rushed to the window in a moment of panic, by the time I got the front half of my body out to see the culprit, he was gone. I went back to Everett, and he wrapped his arms around my neck.

"What do you think he wanted?" he asked.

"I don't know." I looked toward the window again and separated myself from Everett so I could shut it, lock it, and close the curtains.

"We need to be careful," I whispered, wrapping my arms around myself in a feeble attempt to comfort myself.

"We are being careful. And technically speaking, there's no reason to hide anymore."

"Whatever you say. I don't want to be in the

tabloids in the morning, though. I'm still—"

"I know." Sighing, we both thought to ourselves, *I'm still a secret.*

After the sighting at the graduation, I knew that everyone would have figured out mine and Ben's connection by now. It was bound to be all over Twitter and most likely TMZ. I had been a secret kept under wraps for a very good reason—and now that I had been caught locking lips with a band member, well, things wouldn't go over so well for either of us. I didn't want any more trouble, so I decided to kick Everett out of my room. It was the best for the both of us, given our history whenever we were alone.

"You should get some sleep," I said. "We've got a long day ahead of us tomorrow."

He agreed, and I could tell he was resisting the urge to kiss me goodnight, and then he left, shutting my door behind him. I *wanted* him to kiss me goodnight, yet I wanted nothing more than to stay a secret even if only for another day.

While I was getting ready for bed, my phone buzzed. A text message from an anonymous number:

Anonymous: Be careful, little B.

Underneath the caption was a photo—one of Everett and me obviously kissing, his hand on my backside. I hadn't even noticed how low his hand had gotten—though in the picture, it was obvious we were hot for one another. Now I had to think: why did I need to be careful, and who was sending me this anonymous warning?

Anonymous: Goodnight, B.

"Yeah, sleep tight, and don't let the bedbugs bite," I muttered, shutting off my phone for the night. By this time tomorrow, I'd be in a different city in a different state, and I could only hope that everything that was bothering me would leave when I left state lines.

One could only hope.

CHAPTER TWO

The clock on my nightstand indicated it was 3AM. I hadn't been able to sleep at all. It wasn't the noise outside my window, nor was it the aching thought of my missing mother that was lingering inside my head that kept me awake. Instead it was the text message and the photo evidence of Everett and me kissing that accompanied it. The words kept replaying over and over in my head. I had deleted the messages around midnight—though somehow, the words continued to echo in my head.

I sat up, aching to feel something other than what I was feeling then. I had always fought against the instinctual urge to become my mother, and tonight I was done fighting it. I knew what I wanted, and I knew where to get it. I crept quietly into the kitchen, and the only sound that filled the darkness of the box-sized apartment was the soft humming of four boys sleeping in the living room.

Ben was splayed across the couch, Rian and Everett were curled up on the love seat, and Grayson had bravely taken the floor. I tiptoed quietly went to the place where the very thing I wanted was hidden.

In the upper right cabinet, down in the very back, there was a bottle of liquor my mother drank on rare occasions. All her other liquors were in the front—although, the one in the back was by far the strongest. I needed the strength.

I thought back to the first time I saw mother drink. I was eight years old, and Ben was sixteen. He had his first girlfriend, and our mother had caught them in the throes of teenage passion. Now that I think of it, that situation had triggered her to drink in the first place. She had opened a bottle of wine that she had been saving for Christmas dinner, and I had watched her drink the entire thing.

"Frances, never do this to yourself," she had said to me the next morning. "What have I told you about drinking?"

It seemed like she was saying it to me right then. There she was in her white nightdress, her hair a matted mess.

"Mom?" I whispered, and she shook her head. She placed her hands around mine, as if she was trying to grab the bottle (which I brought closer to me), and she giggled in this deranged way that often made me fear for her sanity. She looked at me with wild, bloodshot eyes.

"What do you think you're doing with that, little girl?" she asked, tightening her grip on my hands.

"I'm gonna do what you always do." I opened the twist top cap and held the bottle by the neck.

"You're far too young—it'll kill you," she said, sounding concerned. Her grip tightened further.

"If it'll kill me, then why aren't *you* dead yet?"

23

She ignited with a burning rage when I said this, which led to her yelling, shaking me vigorously.

"You. Will. Not. Speak. To. Me. That. Way!"

I dropped the bottle, which shattered, and everything was happening at accelerating speeds. The lights suddenly were on, and Ben was trying to hold back my mother, who had already slapped me. I barely felt a thing. Everett was guarding me from my mother, and when my mother grabbed a piece of the broken bottle and held it against her pale wrist, Grayson was on the phone with the EMT at once.

I don't know how he did it, but Ben calmed her down to nothing but chest-heaving sobs. When the EMTs arrived, one of them examined my face while the others tended to my mother. My injuries were nothing a little ice couldn't fix. My mother, on the other hand, was in worse shape than I could imagine.

"Ma'am, do you know where you are?"

My mother looked around frantically, shaking her head like a frightened child.

"Do you know who these people are?"

She looked to Everett, Grayson, and Rian and shook her head. She looked at me with a blank expression, shaking her head again. She then looked at my brother, caressed his face and said, "This is my husband."

I tried to hide my tears while Ben had to explain that this wasn't true.

"Mom, I'm...I'm your son. I'm your son, Benjamin." After my mother had been properly sedated, she was put on a gurney, and then they wrapped her up in a blanket for a one-way ride to

Bellevue.

"Will someone stay with Bea?" Ben asked, putting on his coat.

"I'm coming with you," I stated. He looked at me once, and that was all it took for him to realize that, as much as he hated it, I needed to be there too. Despite him trying to avoid the truth, the truth was that I knew more about mother's drinking than he did now. He had been gone for six years, and it had been a long while since I was shielded from our mother's deadly vices.

"Fine, grab a coat and some shoes."

***

My first taste of hospital coffee wasn't my preferred chai latte, but it was strong, and I needed that. I kept thinking of Mackynsie, the text messages, and even my mother. Why was her memory so bad? Why was she so violent? Even though this was something she did often, it still didn't make sense.

I wanted to curl up into a ball so I could disappear. Ben tried to comfort me—although, nothing really could. I was numb inside, and there was no hope left to make me feel whole again.

After what could have easily been hours, a young doctor approached us with a clipboard in his hands.

"Are you here for Jacqueline Morrison?" he asked.

Ben nodded and stood up.

"I believe your mother, Jacqueline, has developed a form of dementia. I need to ask a few questions before I go any further with her treatment."

Ben looked to me then to the doctor. "Go ahead, Doc." He shifted his stance as if preparing for something that would hurt. I tried to pretend that the tar black coffee I was sipping was really a mocha latte from some place other than a hospital.

"Does your mother drink?"

"Yes," Ben answered.

"How often does she drink?"

Ben shrugged, and it dawned on the both of us that he didn't know anymore.

The doctor went on, and Ben didn't know the answers to any of the questions.

"She drinks every day," I said, barely looking up.

The doctor looked to me with concern. "You are?"

"Frances, her daughter."

He started directing the questions toward me.

"How much alcohol does your mother consume daily?"

"On a good day, a little less than half a bottle." Silence filled the room; no one wanted to ask how much she drank on a bad day or what constituted a good day.

"With the information you two gave me, my professional opinion is that your mother has what is called 'Wernicke-Korsakoff Syndrome.'"

Ben asked what it meant.

"It's a form of dementia brought on by excessive substance or alcohol abuse," the doctor explained. He folded his arms over his chest with the clipboard hugging tightly to him. "It's treatable, but I don't know what all has been lost or all of what will be returned. I suggest she immediately go into a rehab facility for treatment."

He handed Ben a few pamphlets for places that could treat our mom and wished us good luck. Ben looked at me, his eyes filled to the brim with despair. When we got home to the mess we had found ourselves in, I couldn't cry anymore. There was nothing left to cry about. I was numb, it was breaking on dawn, and the only thing I wanted was sleep.

Ben hung up his coat on the rack. I stood still until he clamped his hand against my shoulder.

"Get some sleep, Frances. I'll wake you up when it's time to go. Just go get some rest. You'll need it."

With a tired expression, I gave him a nod and dragged myself back to my room. I barely kicked off my shoes and collapsed onto my bed, falling asleep instantly.

It wasn't until I heard the noises of movement and the scent of food being cooked in the kitchen that I woke up. I didn't leave my bed until Ben knocked on my door and opened it a crack.

"Breakfast is ready." he told me. I was sluggish, and I knew that eating something that wasn't frozen or pre-packaged would do me some good.

I walked into the kitchen where the boys were all helping to make breakfast. Once I sat down, I was handed a plate with bacon, eggs, roasted potatoes, and a side of sausage. I was halfway through all of it when my brother set a glass of orange juice next to me.

"I'm glad to know you still have an appetite, Frances," he said, and the boys laughed.

"Yeah, we were afraid you'd become one of those girls who only cared about being thin," Rian said.

"And what if I had?"

He stood silent and let me go on to eat my food.

When I was done eating, I decided to take a shower and style my hair because once I was on the road, showering would become a privilege, and my hair wouldn't be as controlled as it was now.

When I was showered and dressed to my liking and my hair was tamed, the boys were already loading the van outside. Ben took my luggage out for me, and after I finished putting on my makeup, I took one last look at the place. The off-white walls that were dingy with time, the very few framed photos that hung from the wall, my room—it was all so distant already. I was leaving, and I wouldn't be back for six weeks.

I wondered if it was possible to change in six short weeks. I thought that maybe it was, despite what I thought. I knew I was just going to have to find out like anyone else who went on a great adventure. And in my opinion, this was going to be a *damn* good adventure.

***

Arriving at the practice studio, I was surprised to see that everyone was already hard at work. I stifled a yawn, trying to find my place in all the organized chaos. Ben pressed a kiss to my cheek then headed up to the main stage to prepare for practice. As each boy passed me, they waved and smiled at me. I leaned against the snack table and found myself conversing with a guy who had a triple nose piercing.

"I'm Dan," he said when he passed by me to get some food from the snack table. He later told me he was the guitarist for the band that was going to be opening for Eden Sank during the first leg of the tour. His bandmates were breaking down their set so my brother's band could go on, and as they came down from the stage, I got to meet them all. They seemed pretty nice despite all the metal in their faces.

Once Eden Sank went on stage, they played harmoniously. Everything was in sync, and when they came down for a lunch break, while Rian and Grayson were skateboarding in the spacious studio and trying to race one another, I could see someone familiar talking to Everett on stage. He had the same profile and wardrobe choices—the only difference was his hair. It was up in a man-bun, messy, yet well contained. Ben was next to me at the snack table, piling food onto his plate, when I nudged him.

"You can't have my food," he said instantly. I smacked his arm and nodded toward the stage.

"Who is the kid with the man-bun talking to Everett?" I asked, and he nearly snorted.

"That's our summer intern. He goes by Splinter. I can't remember his actual name." My heart started pounding in my chest.

"What's his last name? Do you know?"

"Nightingale," Ben said, and I had to fight the urge to pass out cold. "Why? Do you know him or something? I know you two went to Rosewood together, but—"

"Yeah, I know him."

The way Everett was talking with Splinter, I knew they were getting along.

"Do you not like him or something? Is he secretly an ass? Does he have weird fetishes?"

"No, it's not that. It's just—" I looked to the stage again, and this time, they were both looking at me. I could tell I was the subject of conversation, and it didn't help that they were both pointing toward me. I finally gave in to my weak knees and foggy mind and fell to the ground. Everything around me faded to black.

***

I gradually came to on a velvety soft couch in what appeared to be the green room, and I had bottles of water, juice, and a plate of cookies near my face when I woke up.

"You passed out. The medic said it's a lack of food and a boatload of stress. What do medics know, right?"

I recognized the voice, and when my vision cleared, I looked toward the voice, and there he was: Splinter Nightingale.

"What are you doing here?" I asked him.

"I'm here because I got a cool summer job. What are you doing here?" He held a cookie in front of my face, and since it was an Oreo, I took it eagerly.

"I'm the band leader's sister."

"I know." He smirked. "I just wanted to see if you would come up with some lame excuse."

"Since when do I ever have lame responses?"

He patted his knees and stood. "I was told to watch you until you wake up, and you're awake. I guess my job is done here." He dusted off his knees and looked to me again. "Oh, and we'll be working together throughout the summer, so I hope you can put any high school-ish feelings behind you."

I grabbed his wrist; it was warm and bigger than I had realized. "Wait, I have something I need to say."

He looked at me questioningly.

"You look ridiculous with a man-bun."

He snatched his wrist out of my grip. "I guess the whole 'we're not in high school anymore' doesn't apply to you, Bea," he said and walked out.

As soon as he left, a medic came in, and I was given the all-clear. With a plate full of food and a bottle of juice in my hand, I went back out to the practice arena. It was darkened and the light show, except the pyrotechnics, was on full blast.

I was in such pure awe at my brother's performance and stage presence that I didn't realize that I had been sitting next to Splinter. We watched them for a while, clapping in delight at how good they were. There was awkward silence between changes, but Splinter finally spoke up.

"They're really good."

I glanced at him for a brief moment then looked back to my brother with a smile. "I know."

I sensed Splinter staring at me, and when I turned to look at him, I saw a facial expression I had never seen on him before: disappointment. He opened his mouth to speak, thought better of it, then stood up and leaned down to whisper into my ear.

"That could be you."

He slowly moved away from me and walked to the other side of the room. I know I had *some* musical talent in me. It had to be genetic. I could write decent songs, play piano, and strum a guitar. I was okay on drums and bass, and I even had a decent-sounding voice. But my brother was the star, and the only reason I went to Rosewood was because I had run out of luck with public schools, private schools were becoming too expensive and troublesome, plus Mackynsie and I wanted to be close again. At the time, we had spent a year apart, and it created a huge hole in our friendship. She was going nowhere but up, and I was quickly headed downhill. I knew better, however. She was really sad, and I had a huge problem with punching before thinking. Rosewood accepted me as a student based on my music teacher's high recommendation. To them, I was deemed talented enough to attend Rosewood. When I got there, apparently everyone else thought the same. It wasn't hard rising to the top alongside Mackynsie.

The problem was, on my way to the top, I had somehow lost myself.

I tried to ignore Splinter's words and eat my food while minding my own business. If anyone needed anything to be done, I knew they had Splinter to help. Right now, I was feigning sickness, and I needed my rest. Even if I hadn't passed out, I still needed the rest. We had a lot of places to be within the next six weeks, and being on tour with my brother and the three boys that had seen me grow up was going to be chaotic. Now that Splinter had joined us, things could only be worse.

This was going to be one of the most stressful things I had ever done in my life. If I survived, it would be worth it.

CHAPTER THREE

The first day of tour, which had been dubbed the "Femme Fatale Tour," was finally in full swing. Femme Fatale was a character that had been created by Ben and some of the other members of Eden Sank. It had become a song, then a brand, and now an icon of their band. Femme Fatale meant something different for all of them—though, I didn't really know what it meant for each person. The morning was what I would soon learn was a typical routine: I waited on five boys to finish in the bathroom and shower only to get a cold shower and a messy bathroom space when it was my turn. Did they not understand my need to maintain these curls on my head? I didn't wake up with perfect little ringlets every morning.

When I was done fixing my hair, I attempted to wear minimal makeup: mineral foundation with SPF, as well as regular sunscreen, and my regular dark eyeliner and mascara. I decided to wear a bit of lip balm, and it wasn't until I saw the soft red color smeared on my lips that I realized it was of the tinted variety, so in the end, I had a full face of makeup.

I decided to keep my outfit as simple as possible. High-waisted denim cut-off shorts and a partially buttoned-up flannel shirt that had to date back to the prehistoric era over a white tank top. Add some old and well-loved Converse shoes and I was set. When I was done, everyone had pretty much gone through breakfast, and I chastised them about their lack of chivalry.

"Don't you know that ladies are always first?" I asked. I sat down and ate the last of the bacon and biscuits that were available, and I even scored some OJ.

"When did you finally become a lady, Frances? Was it after the bra riots of 2008, or was there an event we were unaware of?" Rian joked.

After everyone was done talking about the "sick burn" that Rian had doled out, Dean, Eden Sank's tour manager, was going over the schedule for the day. He was only about halfway through when I realized it was jam-packed. When he finished talking with the band, he took Splinter and me aside to talk about our duties as the on-the-road interns. We were on roadie duty, and on retainer for everything else. Splinter's main responsibility was the drums, and I was fetching towels and water bottles for the rock stars all day. Simple enough, right?

"Frances, you guys about ready?" Rian asked impatiently.

"Yeah!" I shouted back into the bus.

First stop on the itinerary was a radio station. They would be playing their mid-afternoon hour show, and the radio station was giving away a select amount of last-minute tickets to the sold-out show in Jersey City.

The boys mainly joked around and hung out like real friends until they were called back into the recording station. Splinter and I were allowed back there with them, and once they were announced over the radio waves, they played their song, "Femme Fatale." After they were done, the radio hosts, L. Tinsley and Big Poppa, asked a lot of different questions about the tour and about the songs they chose for this particular album.

"What influenced the Femme Fatale character that eventually led to a Top 100 single, ten million copies of your album sold, and a big tour to boot?" L. Tinsley asked, and the boys laughed.

"You could say Femme Fatale is a woman that combines our worst fears, our insecurities, and even a few of our worst nightmares combined into a character," Ben explained. "What started out as a way to vent brought out a song, and then an entire album, and now this tour. It's amazing what you can do when you use your fears for positive means."

I smiled proudly at my brother—though, he didn't see it, focused as he was on the interview, which I understood.

""Femme Fatale" has been such a big hit. What's next? What will Eden Sank do after this tour is over?" Big Poppa asked.

"Right now we're all doing a bit of writing and brainstorming. I can't say whether or not there will be a new album right off the bat, but I can say we will be working behind the scenes," Ben said.

"We will be working to find the next best thing," Rian chimed in.

"Hopefully I'll finally marry my girlfriend," Grayson joked, and we all laughed.

After a few more questions, they played another song, and we were off the air for at least three minutes. Ben looked over to me with a soft smile, and I smiled back. We took photos with L. Tinsley and Big Poppa for the radio's social media sites, and once the photos were posted, I had to turn the notifications off on my phone. Every few seconds, the photos I was tagged in were getting likes and comments.

I could tell my brother was acting as if this was the most natural thing in the world. He wasn't bothered by the constant notifications or the fact that he was never really left alone. He appeared to enjoy the never-ending attention. All I could think of was a time when he barely wanted to be looked at. Now he was the center of attention, and he was loving it. Was it because he had come out of his shell? He seemed more confident now than he had been the last time I had seen him.

As the day went on and we went from place to place, I kept bumping into Splinter. Literally. We were always in the other's way or annoying each other. I could probably rip his head off if he made one more snarky comment, and I think he felt the same about me.

When it was time for the show to start, we were in our places.

"You're really annoying," he said, standing next to me.

"I could say the same about you," I retorted.

"Yeah, but like, you really don't care about anyone except yourself."

I glanced at him curiously. I didn't question what he meant. The more I thought about it, the less I wanted to know.

***

Each opening band blazed through their sets, and when it came time to join Eden Sank for their prayer circle, I felt even closer to my brother than I ever had growing up. I hadn't thought that was possible. Seeing him in his circle of trust right before his big opening number and being able to witness it made me feel a part of his life again. He gave me a hug and a kiss on the cheek and went rushing off to go on stage with the wild, screaming fans behind barricades. Watching my brother and his friends perform, I was filled with awe. Everyone else was excited—though, they seemed okay with it as if this spectacular performance I had witnessed was nothing more than a mundane turnout or an everyday occurrence.

Passing each boy a towel and a bottle of water, I watched their rituals unfold. Rian threw the towel over his left shoulder and immediately guzzled the entire bottle of water. Grayson wiped his face gently with the towel and used his water bottle to cool off. Ben doused himself in cold water then proceeded to wipe himself dry. Everett did neither. He looked at me with stunned eyes as if he hadn't really seen me until that moment.

"Take your stuff and go, rock star," I said, handing him the towel and water bottle. He took them with a smile and passed me by. He didn't need to say another word to me; I knew exactly what he was thinking.

I went back into the green room to see a huge party setting up. Alcohol, obvious drug paraphernalia, and scantily clad girls everywhere...I felt more and more out of place, and the way Everett and all the other boys took to it, it made me wonder if this was what it was all about for them.

***

The party was in full swing, and I had been moved around more than a hot potato. Splinter appeared as uncomfortable as I was—although, he was being moved between various women—I had a feeling that he didn't mind that part so much. I wanted something to drink, so I got up to go to the drink table and found myself facing one of the band groupies. I had never really imagined my brother had groupies. Things had changed since the last time I saw him. He was lusted after by a lot of women (and men), so he probably had sex with whomever he wanted and whenever he wanted. I really had to accept that he was grown up; he wasn't a kid anymore.

"Who are you?" asked a badly bleached blonde woman sipping on a cocktail of some sort.

"What does it matter?" I asked with obvious annoyance.

"You look too young to be in here," she said,

smacking her lips. It was annoying. In fact, her face alone annoyed me.

"I'm old enough to be wherever I damn well please," I snapped then Everett pulled me back. Seeing him had a calming effect on me.

"What do you think you're doing?" he asked me, his speech slightly slurred.

"I'm trying to find something to drink. What do you think you're doing?"

He shrugged. "I'm doing what I always do."

"What's that, getting majorly faded?" I asked, peering through the thin screen of smoke that separated us. He was far gone, and I knew it. I wanted to see if a part of the guy I knew to be real was still in there beneath all the drugs and alcohol.

"Frances, don't mind this. This is who *I am*. Roll with it." He tried to kiss me, but I pushed him away.

"Don't kiss me, not while you're like this." I had my hand on his chest, and he grabbed my hand in his, throwing it aside as if it was a piece of trash.

"Bea, if I can accept that you've got flaws, why can't you accept mine?" He was raising his voice, and despite the loud music, people were taking notice of our fight.

The next thing I knew, I was getting water dumped all over me, and I screamed out from the shock of the sudden wet and cold.

"What the hell?" I screeched.

"Cool off, kiddo. This is no place for a baby like yourself." It was the same blonde, and she had dumped the last of the water on me. How ironic.

"You're going to pay for that!" I shouted. No one could stop me from lunging at her. She didn't do much to fight me off—though, when Ben caught sight of us, he appeared angrier that I was starting brawls rather than the fact that some groupie was messing with me. He dragged me off of the girl and kicked her out.

"Yeah, just pick your favorite groupies. You're all the same!" she shouted as she was escorted from the party.

"I'm not a groupie!" I yelled.

I could tell Ben was disappointed in me without him having to say a single word.

When things had calmed down, I found a shot of tequila that was sitting out by itself. The most logical thing would be to leave it be, but I wasn't the most logical person on the planet. I took the shot glass filled with liquid amber, and I swallowed it down. The burning sensation traveling down my throat didn't bother me at all. So I drank another, and another, and another. I drank until I was dizzy and numb from the inside out. I wanted to find Everett to see if he liked me this way, drunk and incapacitated as he had been. I wanted to see if when my flaws matched his, if he still wanted to kiss me. I couldn't find him. I couldn't find Splinter or Ben either. Rian was still partying hard, and when I walked out of the green room, I saw that Grayson was on the phone with his fiancé.

"Babe, I'll talk to you later. I've got to help someone get back to the bus. Yeah, you know how these parties get. I love you." He grabbed me by the wrist and led me back to the safety of the tour bus.

"I can't believe you're drunk right now, Bea," he said sternly. "What did you have to drink?"

"Tequila."

"Ah, the good stuff. Rest up. We'll be back here soon enough."

He left me on the bus by myself, and went back outside to the venue to catch up with the other boys who were still partying hard.

Somehow, I found a way to change out of my dampened clothes and into clean, dry pajamas. Then, I crawled into my bunk. I curled up underneath the blankets and buried my face into the fluffy pillow Ben had gotten me, promptly falling asleep.

The next morning, I woke up with a killer headache and instant regret. When I got up, coffee and other breakfast items had been set out, and all the boys were sitting in the lounge with a groggy look on their faces. I didn't say a word to anyone, got a French toast stick and a piece of bacon, and sat down. I could tell there was plenty to be said when the time was right. Since Dean was in the middle of reprimanding everyone, I decided it was a good time to check my phone. There were plenty of notifications: photos which I needed to untag and photos I didn't want anyone to see. There was one text message, and it filled me with a new sense of fear.

Anonymous: Too much fun can lead to many troubles. Watch out, B.

It was another anonymous message, and this time, there was a picture of me knocking back tequila shots. Shocked, I quickly deleted the messages and the pictures, trying to act natural.

Dean left to go figure out some logistics for the next leg of the tour. The boys didn't have a typical reaction to my post-party hangover. They weren't angry with me for drinking, and instead, I was the butt of all of their jokes. I was okay with this and tried to laugh at all the bad jokes they came up.

At the same time, my mind wandered over to the messages I had been receiving. Who would possibly send me those messages? Who had enough of an agenda against me to try and scare me the way this person was attempting to?

Everett looked different this morning. He looked angry. I wanted to know what was on his mind, so when he got up to go to the bathroom, I followed him, much to his frustration.

"Frances, let me through," he said as I blocked the bathroom door.

"No, not until you tell me why you've been acting so weird." He tried dodging me, and I proved quicker than he was, even while fending off a hangover. He was pretty sluggish this morning, and even though I knew it was partially due to a hangover, alcohol wasn't the only thing that I could smell from the stench of his sweat.

"What did you do last night? Huh? You normally don't act like that."

"Frances, would you let me pee, goddammit!" He shoved me to the side. I was so shocked by his use of force I stared in disbelief at the bathroom door he slammed shut in my face.

Shaking my head, I went back over to the lounge area where everyone was giving me weird stares.

"Everett is acting weird," I said.

"Bea, he is acting weird to *you*, but to him, he is acting completely normal. Things have changed for all of us since the last time we saw you," Rian said.

I didn't have the time to argue once Everett came back. He sat down next to Splinter, acting as if nothing had happened between us.

"Can someone pass the bacon?" he asked. I obliged and took a piece off of the plate. From the looks of it, he was ready to argue with everything and everyone today.

The way Everett was acting indicated how angry he was. The way he chewed, sipped, and did everything was angry. It was so odd, and even the rest of the band was taking notice. Everett was the kindest guy on the planet. He'd never seemed to have an angry bone in his body, but now I could see that had changed.

While we were waiting for the lunch stop during our driving, I was able to hang out with Ben in the back of the bus and talk. It was nice, and I started to realize that he hadn't really changed that much. He was still goofy and awkward, and he still wanted something to cuddle with at night. I tried my best to keep up with all the things he was telling me. All the breakups and relationships I had missed, all the memories he had made without me—there was so much I had missed out on since I was still in school.

"So what about you? Is there anything you want to share with me?" he asked.

There was plenty I wanted to share with him, but I didn't know where to begin. I tried to talk about Mackynsie, which proved difficult. I wanted to tell him how I had lost my virginity—though, I figured that he wouldn't appreciate that story. Heck, the experience wasn't that great to begin with—why would I want to go around sharing it?

"So, when I was applying to colleges," I told him, "I decided to major in music production."

"Really?" he asked with great interest.

I nodded, and he smiled.

"You'll be great, Frances, I'm sure of it."

"Thanks, bro." I hugged him, and I didn't know how I felt about sharing that with him now that I had.

It was weird, and seemed as if it were incomplete, as if there was more that I was supposed to share with him about it. Was I supposed to tell him how I came to the choice to major in music? Did I tell him how I landed all the scholarships for the music major? I had no clue, but I knew that for now my brother was happy, and for the moment, I felt normal. That was all I wanted: to feel normal.

CHAPTER FOUR

It was day six of tour, and we were headed to Lexington, Kentucky. Personally, I found nothing interesting about Kentucky until I learned there was a statue of Superman in the town square of one of the cities we'd be going through. That made it a little more bearable.

I was still worried about Everett. He had gotten better, but he still wasn't himself. Every time I approached him, I felt like I was bothering him, so I never got around to asking what had happened to make him so angry. I don't think anyone wanted to know or to ask.

When the others were getting breakfast, I was doing my hair. Being on tour hadn't done it any favors, and the curls were a mess. I looked like a deranged poodle. Thankfully, I knew a few tricks to manage it—though, I doubted I would have enough bobby pins to last me the whole tour. Or contacts, for that matter.

"Hey, has anyone seen my box of contacts?" I called into the bus. No one had. Then I got to thinking…Everett. He hated the contacts. Would he have thrown them away? Though I was unsure, it was worth asking. When he passed by the bathroom, I caught his arm, and it felt foreign, like I was touching a stranger.

"What is it, Frances?" he asked after a moment of silence.

"Yeah, uhm…have you seen my contacts?" I asked him, trying to sound as sweet and nice as possible.

"Yeah, I think I saw them in the trash back in Charleston."

My eyes grew wide—Charleston, West Virginia was a whole city ago, a whole state away.

"What have we done with the trash from Charleston?" I asked.

He shrugged. "I suppose we left it there."

He walked off, and I about lost it. I couldn't believe how cool and collected he was about the whole thing. He may have liked my eyes, but that didn't mean he could just let my expensive contact lenses go into the trash!

"Everett Graham Thompson! I don't believe you!" I shouted, and everyone, including Splinter, looked at us.

"Why? I didn't do anything," Everett replied, and I was ready to blow a gasket.

"You did too! You knew my contacts were in the trash by mistake, and you left them there! Why would you do that?"

His anger was flaring up again, and I could tell he was fighting it. I didn't want to add to the flames, but I was angry—and when I was angry, everyone had to deal with it.

47

"Everett, just because you don't like something I do—"

"Just because you don't like something about yourself doesn't mean you cover it up!" he cut in.

"Who said I didn't like it? I never said that!"

"It was all over your face when I mentioned it back in New York!"

"You're reading way too much into this!"

"And *you're* reading too much into *this!*"

Splinter took me back into the bathroom and said, "Finish getting ready. You can wear your glasses if you need to."

I rolled my eyes. "They weren't prescription." He appeared confused by this, so I pointed to my left eye. "It's called a partial heterochromia iridium. A sectoral heterochromia. One section of my eye is a different color than the rest." He looked intrigued.

"That's pretty cool," he said. "I was always wondering why you had different colored eyes during different days of the week."

"Well, it's fun that way. Wait, you noticed my eyes?" I asked self-consciously.

"Yeah, I mean you're beautiful. Your eyes are killer. Forces I can't control pull me into them. If looks could kill, your eyes would be murderers." He looked embarrassed then by his enthusiasm. "Yeah, just hurry up and finish getting ready. We're getting breakfast at a diner." He went off after that, and it left me with a lot to think about.

My eyes are killer? My eyes could be murderers?

Was he insane, or was he smitten? Every time I looked back over at Everett, I wished my eyes could kill. Specifically, I wish they could kill *him*.

***

We were sitting in a private room in a diner in Lexington. It was usually used for parties, but we wanted some alone time away from the fans. Normally, Ben was okay with them asking for autographs and pictures, but today, he wasn't in such a giving mood. I could understand that. I wouldn't want to be bombarded by people who wanted nothing but a picture or a signature every day.

By the time we had gotten to the diner, they had stopped serving breakfast and were starting the lunch shift. This was okay with me, since their lunch menu looked more promising than their breakfast menu did. When we were done ordering, we sat around the table in silence.

Dean, the tour manager, was preoccupied with his tablet, and Ben was more focused on the little napkin he was writing on. Grayson was on the phone with his fiancé, Lydia. Rian was texting some girl, and I could see him laughing with joy, something I didn't witness very often.

"Careful, Rian. With the way that girl has you laughing, she'll have you buying rings," I mentioned, and he shook his head.

"I'm never going to settle down."

"Never say never," everyone said at once.

I took a look at Everett, who had only smiled for a moment. I wanted to ask him something, but I couldn't get over the fact that Splinter was shaking his leg underneath the table. I went to kick his foot to make him stop when I noticed he was staring awkwardly at his hands in his lap. I let him go on with what he was doing after that. I continued to watch everyone around me because it intrigued me. Boys I hadn't seen in six years were suddenly men, and there was a kid from high school I barely knew that seemed to notice me more than I noticed him.

This is why I was a people watcher. As an observer of people, you often find them doing little things that make you question what *you're* doing when you think no one is watching. It made me think of how Splinter had noticed my eyes when I didn't notice him at all. He was at the bottom of the food chain at Rosewood, and I was at the top. With all of these things in my mind, I was getting up to go to the bathroom when our food came, as well as an old acquaintance of Ben's, K.L. James.

"Hello, you guys. Boy, have you grown since I've last seen you," he said. "Beatrice, is that you? Wow, what a beauty."

"K.L., what a surprise," Ben said. He was trying to sound pleasant, except it was really hard for him today.

"I know I dropped in uninvited," K.L. said. "I heard about your show tonight, and I happened to see your bus around back when I was driving by. I thought I'd come in and say hello to some old friends."

K.L. James was a famous music producer. He'd signed Ben and Eden Sank in their early days—though, it hadn't really worked out. K.L. was previously known for his punk-rock influences and his way around a distraught, grungy crowd. When he signed Ben and the band, he was going for a more pop sounding machine. Ben hadn't liked it, and they'd split ways. After six unproductive months, trying to find a label that would take them once they'd been with K.L James was hard. It hadn't worked out well, and things had gotten a bit harder for them after that. Obviously not for long.

"Beatrice, may I borrow you for a moment?" K.L. asked me.

"Uhm, sure." Halfway through my sandwich, I wiped my mouth and hands and walked with K.L to the back of the room where we couldn't be heard.

"Beatrice," he started. He never called me Frances, or Bea—just Beatrice. "I want to see how you feel about signing on with me for a publishing deal. If I remember correctly, you're quite the songwriter, and you've got a good voice. What have you been doing with that since I last saw you?"

Last time I saw him, I was twelve. I didn't think the songs I wrote were good, but I thought that I had an okay voice.

"I'm not interested," I said. "I'm going to college in the fall, and I won't have time for outside activities."

"Ah, yes. You're attending Dartmouth on a music scholarship. Tell me, what are you planning on doing with a degree in music?"

"You've been stalking me, haven't you?" Despite my joking tone, my words stung more than I intended.

"Maybe I have, but for good reason. You went to Rosewood Academy, and that, my dear, is a great academy for budding artists."

"Like I said, I'm not interested." I left him

standing there and went back to the table to finish my lunch.

"What did K.L want?" Ben asked.

"To congratulate me on graduating from Rosewood."

Ben nodded, and I was glad he couldn't see the deception in my eyes.

When we got to the venue for the dress rehearsal, I was already feeling tension between Splinter and me, the last thing I needed. I felt vulnerable, and maybe he saw that too and was ready to attack. Would he attack? I couldn't be sure. Maybe he wasn't that kind of guy to attack a girl when she was down; although, I didn't know Splinter like I knew everyone else.

I knew the basics. He wore a man-bun, skinny jeans, Vans, and douche-y V-necks. He was a total hipster and wouldn't even admit to it. Maybe that was why I despised him so much. Either way, I knew that we had to get along for this whole internship to work. I wanted it to work.

This would be the last I saw of him. After this summer was over, I was going to Dartmouth, and he was going wherever he was going next. We would never cross paths again. I didn't know how I was supposed to feel about that. If Mackynsie were here, she would tell me to be thankful.

While I was working backstage later that evening, I heard a few new guests entering the premises. One was K.L., and the other was Ella Green. Ella Green was well known for her publicity stunts and her YouTube videos. Although I had never seen one, I was pretty sure she was here to interview the band. As for K.L., he was here for the same reason he was at the diner where we had lunch: to reel me into his world. I refused, knowing that wouldn't stop him from trying again.

"Frances, can you take Ms. Green and Mr. James to the green room?" one roadie asked me. I threw the towel I was haphazardly folding to the side, and I went to guide Ella and K.L. to the green room.

When we got there, Ben was celebrating something, and he wanted me to hear it. He showed me the invitation that had been waiting for them when they got here. It was for the American Music Awards in November, and when I saw that he and the band were nominated for an award, I was just as giddy with excitement as the whole lot of them. Ben and I hugged and jumped up and down, squealing in excitement.

After we came back to our senses I said, "Oh, guys, Ella Green and K.L are here." The sound of Ella's name struck a fire in Ben. Not a good fire either.

"Is something wrong?" I asked.

Ella was suddenly screaming at Ben. I was so confused, and so when Ella kept yelling, I yelled over her.

"Shut up! What the hell is going on?" I asked.

Ben waved his hand, signaling that I should leave this alone, and I ignored him.

"Don't you know?" Ella said. "I wanted to date the wonderful Ben Morrison, but he refused. He *refused!* Like, who refuses to date *me*? I'm *Ella Green* for Christ's sake. I'm the mother—"

"It's time to shut up, Ella. I can see your ego

loud and clear." She gasped at my comment, more enraged that I even spoke to her during her outburst than the fact that my brother had refused her invitation.

"Who are you? Like, what are you even doing here? You were folding towels when I came in— you're a little, good for nothing—"

It was a reflex, and I mean it when I say this— but I punched her in the nose. Usually I'm pretty good at controlling my anger, and other times I don't realize how angry I am, and my reflexes take over. She was wailing like a child and holding her head back as she stumbled around as if my punch to her nose had debilitated her ability to maintain her balance.

"Dammit, Frances! Do you know who she is?" Ben was yelling at me now, and I didn't know how to react. He was rushing to get towels and ice for Ella.

After a medic checked her nose and said it was fine, she was escorted off the premises, all the while shouting about how I was going to pay for this. I was like a child stuck in the time out corner when Ben came back. My arms were wrapped around myself for safety, and I hung my head in shame.

"What are you doing, Bea? Do you want to get us into trouble? She's a YouTube star. She could easily post a rant about this and make it go viral overnight!"

It was time to prepare for the show, and I tried to leave, except Ben wouldn't stop yelling.

"Frances, if you keep screwing things up the way you are, I'm going to regret ever bringing you on this tour! How can I show the world how wonderful my sister is if she keeps acting like a whiny, spoiled brat with an uncontrollable right hook?"

I could tell Everett was about to call him out on his behavior, but I shot him a look that told him not to.

"I'm sorry, Ben, it won't happen again. I'll go back to folding towels." I had never been so isolated and demeaned in my life. So much for sibling love.

***

The show was a success as usual—though, when I joined everyone on the bus that night, it was obvious there had been a shift among the people on it. I felt so horrible that I didn't know what to do. Though it was obvious Everett was still angry with me, he wanted to help me with Ben. Ben was angry with me and kept as far away from me as he could on the bus. He was obsessively checking Ella Green's YouTube channel in hopes that she didn't post a video about the incident. I was hoping she didn't either, but she had said I was going to pay—and that could be any number of things to a girl with a camera and an Internet following. I knew things were different between my brother and me now. When he looked at me, it wasn't with the love and affection I usually got from him—it was with anger and disgust. I wanted to tell him that family was more important than a silly threat from a silly girl—though, I had a feeling his reputation was more important than his family at this point. How the world saw him affected him so much.

When I went to my bunk that night, I checked YouTube as well. Before I could even see if any new uploads had made it to my feed, I saw another anonymous text.

> *Anonymous: You're being very naughty, B. You best control your temper; it'll get you nowhere. How is paying that debt coming along?*

The first thing that came to my mind was: I'm being stalked. I'm being stalked.

I'm being stalked.

CHAPTER FIVE

Fourteen cities, three weeks, eight break days out of the fourteen sold-out shows. This was the life of a rock star. Except, I didn't get all the perks. Ben still wasn't really talking to me, and Everett was still giving me a hard time. All I had left was Splinter, and he wasn't exactly my idea of good company.

It was the last night of the first leg, and everyone was on edge. We were traveling back to NYC from Rapid City, South Dakota. We were flying this time, and we were supposed to have a day full of shows. One would be held in a small music shop, and another would be at Madison Square Garden. After the New York show was over, we would be going on our one-week break for the holidays. Technically, we were given five days—although due to the Fourth of July, we had two extra free days. After our vacation, we would be back at it again, and the West Coast of the United States was expecting us for the second leg of the tour.

Despite my feeble attempts at apologizing to Ben for punching Ella in the nose, he wasn't easing up on being a brat to me.

Ella Green never posted a video, Snapchat, Instapic, or Tweet about the incident, which proved to me she was more bark than bite. This didn't help me like I thought it would, though. I guess Ben was angry with me for more than my nose-punching reflex, and I had no clue what else I could have possibly done to piss him off.

Most of our trip was silent. When we landed at JFK International Airport and were heading toward the streets, I was relieved.

Ben and I had a driver who was picking us up. Splinter had his family come get him for his break. Grayson's fiancé, Lydia, and their daughter, who'd just turned nine, met him at the airport. Rian also had a driver, and Everett had his brother Ryker pick him up.

Since Ben and I had started fighting, Everett and I had sort of made up. When I say "made up," I mean when we weren't bickering with one another; we were making out until our anger toward each other melted. It made a huge difference, yet it made me feel as if I was hiding something important from everyone else on the bus. I didn't know if we were ever going to tell my brother and the band that we were a thing. Were we a thing? I couldn't really tell where we had drawn the line.

I said goodbye to everyone and climbed into a van with Ben to go to the Marriott Hotel, where we would have separate rooms. Ben said he wanted to be by himself to write, kind of like Splinter wanted time by himself after being on a bus with me for nearly four weeks. Everyone was doing their own thing. Me? I was going to be stuck alone with my own thoughts. I was planning on being able to get out and roam the city streets like I always did— though at this point, I knew it would be hard to leave while remaining unnoticed. Even though Ben wanted his alone time to write, he always had a sense of when I was about to cause trouble for him.

When we got to the hotel, Ben was getting into his writing mode—he was frustrated and angsty, and I was getting ready to go out on the town. He wouldn't even know I was gone.

I dressed in a pair of high-waisted shorts, a faded white muscle tank with the Coca-Cola logo on it that I had cut into a crop top, and navy blue low-top Converse. To block the wind, I put on a yellow cardigan. My hair was up in a ponytail, except you could barely tell with all the curls and frizz. I was hoping the frizz would go down, but it was New York, and it was humid. I grabbed my hotel key and put it in my back pocket, as well as my phone, then left the hotel room.

Once I was outside in the streets, I was able to walk down the busy sidewalk with the millions of other busy people. It helped get all the thoughts out of my head, and I was able to calm down quite a bit. I felt like I had been cooped up too much lately. Even though we had eight free days, I rarely got to leave the bus. Mostly that was by my own choice since I didn't want to cause a scene in public with my brother or anyone else who was angry with me at the time. Now, I was at home in the city, and I was going to set myself free. I knew Ben wanted to talk to me later tonight, and I was nervous about that. I was guessing he wanted to talk about Mother or about the incident with Ella. *Whatever* he wanted to talk about, I knew it was going to be something I didn't want to hear.

***

I had just sat down for lunch in a little back-alley bistro when I got a text from Everett, asking to meet him. I knew he didn't want to meet in public, rather in a secretive location. I was okay with this. I didn't want anyone to know about us if they didn't have to. Especially Ben, I *really* didn't want him to know just yet. I didn't know what to call the relationship between Everett and me, so how could I be okay with letting everyone else know if I didn't have a clue?

I knew that the air of attraction was strong between Everett and me. It had been since I was sixteen. But I wasn't sixteen anymore, and I definitely wasn't the same person he found himself under the covers with for one night. Though that didn't change how he felt about me. Maybe he hadn't gotten the full taste of who I had become, or maybe he refused to acknowledge the change at all.

When I paid for my lunch and went on my way, I decided to call Everett to ask where he wanted to meet up.

"Hey," I said when he picked up.

"What is it?" he said quickly.

"Where do you want to meet?" I asked with a nervous laugh.

"Oh, right. How about your apartment? Is it still

yours?"

"I guess we'll find out." I wasn't sure if Ben had been paying the landlord to keep a vacant apartment open for me. Once we got there and found that the locks hadn't been changed and everything still looked the same, we knew that there had been some sort of deal to keep it open.

I didn't have a single second to collect my thoughts once Everett kissed me. It was filled with a passion I never really knew he was capable of. His hands groped every curvature of my body, and soon enough clothes were coming off, leaving a trail to my bedroom. We fell back on the bed, which I hadn't slept in for weeks.

It was almost odd doing this. Why was Everett all over me? I pulled away from his lips and pushed a hand against his chest.

"Everett, what are you doing?" I asked him, trying to catch my breath.

"What do you think?" He pressed another kiss to my lips as if to shut me up. I pushed him off of me and sat up, using my elbows for support against the bed.

"Everett, I thought we were supposed to—"

"I know what we were supposed to do, but I know how I feel, Frances. I love you. I don't want to be without you."

"Everett, I don't know how I'm supposed to feel about that."

I had never been in love, nor had I ever thought about what love would feel like. I always assumed that you would know it when you loved someone; it would come as a second nature, as an instinctual desire. I didn't feel that way with Everett, and I didn't know what I was supposed to tell him.

"You're supposed to feel—dammit, I can't tell you what you're supposed to feel, Frances. Just tell me you love me too. Tell me you feel the same way."

I stared at him, trying to imagine myself marrying him, having his kids, growing old together. I couldn't do it. I knew I loved Everett—though, it wasn't in the way I was supposed to. Not in the way he needed me to.

"Everett, I don't feel the same way."

He slowly pulled himself away from me, and I could see him unwinding from the inside out. His mind and his heart were unraveling from the words I had so carelessly spewed out of my mouth. I was his Femme Fatale. I knew that now, and I couldn't believe that I had just broken his heart.

"Everett, please." I wanted to stop him; in fact, I tried. He was too fast, and I was too slow when it came to redressing myself.

***

When I arrived back at the hotel, K.L. James was coming out of the elevator. Naturally, I ducked and hid from his view. He looked rather odd. When he was gone, I went back up to my room, where Ben was waiting for me.

"Where have you been?" he asked, his arms crossed over his chest.

"I've been out. Why?" He opened the door to my room and made me go inside. When I did, he shut the door behind him and let out an earful.

"How could you lie to me about K.L.? How could you not tell me about him trying to scout you? Frances Beatrice Morrison, I am beyond furious with you! How could you do this to me? To the band? I am in complete shock right now—I can't—I can't deal with this."

"Don't blame me for something I didn't ask for! Don't go around acting all hurt because I didn't tell you! I didn't tell you because I didn't want the deal. I wanted nothing to do with him after what he put you through! I don't know what he said to you. He eats bullshit for breakfast! Ben, you're my brother, and I am tired of fighting with you. Can we please stop and pretend that everything is all right between us?"

There was a moment of silence between us then a knock on the door. There was a pregnant pause between Ben and me, and when a second knock disturbed the silence, Ben told me in a rigid tone, "Just answer it."

I did as I was asked and opened the door to find Splinter standing awkwardly in the doorway.

"What are you doing here?" I snapped, using my tone of voice and hard facial expression to make it obvious that this wasn't the best of times.

"I was trying to get a break from my family, and I was told to fetch Ben. There's a problem he needs to take up with management. That's all they told me."

"We'll finish this later," Ben said. He stormed out of the room, leaving me in a wind of guilt and frustration. This also left Splinter and me alone.

To make matters worse, I got another anonymous text. It was a picture of Everett and me back in the apartment. I couldn't hide the shock from my face when I read it, and Splinter was quick to start asking questions.

"What's the matter, Bea?"

I shook my head, trying to think. Why was this happening? Who was behind it? What could they possibly gain from this?

"Bea, what's going on?" Splinter tried to grab my phone to see what had me so shocked. I snatched it away which led to being chased by Splinter around my room, trying to figure out why I was so freaked out.

"Something is going on, and it's starting to show. What the hell is happening, Bea?"

"Why don't you mind your own business, Splinter?"

I managed to dodge him and tried to exit the room. He squeezed in between me and the door and blocked me from escaping.

"Bea, tell me what you're hiding."

I went back to my suitcase where I decided to change for tonight's show.

"Bea, you're worrying me. Please tell me what's going on?"

"I'm going to change for the shows tonight. Are you going to stick around for that?"

"When are you going to decide that it's easier to let people in than it is to push them out, Bea?" he said. "You can't do everything on your own. I know Mackynsie was your friend, but there are more people in this world than one pretty blonde girl who cared more about popularity than she did her best friend."

I stared at him with tears in my eyes. "Get out!" I shouted. "Get out now, or I'll call security!"

I physically pushed him out the door, and once it was locked and when I was sure he was gone, I resumed dressing myself, unable to stop the tears. However, the show had to go on.

The show at Mixed Records Shop was a success. I had to hide myself skillfully in order to avoid getting run over by the stampede of fans who had come to the in-store show and signing. I still wasn't able to talk to Ben, and that was primarily due to the fact that in between the time we had been interrupted and the time it took to get ready for the show, there'd been no time available for us to continue our argument.

***

I was sitting in the back of a van with Splinter after the show. Rian and Grayson were in front of us, and Everett was sitting in the front with Ben. The tension surrounding Splinter and me was making me uncomfortable. He wanted to know what was going on with me, and at the same time, he wanted to be angry with me for not telling him. I couldn't really tell him anything at this point. When we caught ourselves staring at each other during the silent ride to Madison Square Gardens, I thought of the words he spewed at me in the hotel room about Mackynsie. They hurt like a venomous bite to my being, and yet a part of me wondered if there was truth beyond the pain I sensed in his words.

Going to Madison Square Gardens had always been a dream of Ben's, and now that he would be playing there for the last show on this leg of this tour, he was beyond happy. It was as if everything else that had happened tonight was irrelevant.

Watching the boys take the stage that night was different. They were filled with pride, with joy. They were going to close with "Femme Fatale," and I knew that tonight I was that woman to more than one person in the band.

Every night they played was the same— screaming fans, sweaty boys, and pure joy emitting from each person. Tonight was no different. The fans reacted the same as they did in any other arena, and the boys left the stage with a feeling of accomplishment. There were parties, and there was booze, something I had learned was a staple in rock star life. Everything was going as it normally would, at least until I spotted Crosley. He had gotten a special pass from his friend's uncle to come backstage. As much as I tried to avoid him, there was no hiding myself from him. He could spot me from a million miles away. I wanted nothing more than to duck and hide like I had with K.L., but there was nowhere to hide backstage.

"My, my, my. Bea, what a surprise." He knew who my brother was; he shouldn't have been so shocked to see me here. "You're looking great. The first month of no school has done you well."

I rolled my eyes and muttered thanks.

"How has touring treated you? Surely you don't always look so pretty like you do today."

I wanted nothing more than to punch him in the face, but I kept my cool. "No, it isn't always easy. I manage." I was looking around for anyone or anything that could take me away from Crosley, and there was no help in sight.

"Do you remember our little talk?" he asked, wrapping a hand gently around my wrist.

"Depends, which one?" I asked, trying to keep my eyes scanning across the room.

He chuckled into my ear, and it sent goose bumps down my spine. "About the debt you owe me."

My eyes grew wide, and my mind was reeling back to the messages. Was Crosley the person who had been stalking me all summer? He let go of my wrist and checked the time.

"Oh, well look. Time sure does fly. I hope the rest of your summer goes well. Until next time, Bea." He bowed and went on his way.

I was left shaking, and as much as I tried to hide it, everyone seemed to notice.

"Bea, are you cold?" Grayson asked, offering me his jacket, which I took without arguing.

I went outside to the cab that was to take Ben and me back to the hotel. Right when I thought I was ready to escape, Splinter caught up with me.

"Bea, wait up!"

"What is it, Splinter?"

"What was Crosley doing talking to you?"

I shrugged. "Just reminiscing," I said even though I knew that wasn't the case.

"You're a horrible liar." He shook his head and laced his fingers together behind his head. "I know

67

something when I see it, Bea. I'm going to figure it out even if it's the death of me."

I got into the cab. "I've got to go." I shut the door, and the cabbie took off. My phone vibrated in my pocket, and I pulled it out to check. Another anonymous message and this time it held more of a threat.

Anonymous: Pay your dues, or I'll find a way to get rid of you.

"Everything okay?" Ben finally asked.

I looked over at him and locked my phone. "Yeah, everything's great," I lied.

CHAPER SIX

The whole week I spent at the hotel was agonizing. I wanted nothing more than to cool off and get things right with my brother. I knew it wouldn't be easy, and today was our last day—the Fourth of July. We were all supposed to go to Coney Island to see the fireworks, and then we were headed off for the second leg of the tour.

I dressed in a pair of denim shorts to go with my Green Day's American Idiot logo tank and an American Flag bandana wrapped around my wrist. While I was doing my makeup, someone knocked on the door.

"Come in," I called. I noticed it was Ben.

He smiled at me. "You look great. Real American." I laughed, and so did he. That was the first time in a long time we had laughed together.

"Ben, I—"

He shook his head and cut me off. "I have something to tell you, so please sit down and listen."

I sat on the edge of my hotel bed. "Okay, I'm listening."

He started pacing back and forth. "Bea, I'm sorry

I've been such an ass. It isn't you—it's me. It's me, and it's...I've been seeing someone, and not just any someone—someone I had to keep a secret. I didn't want to, but they wanted me to."

I nodded, encouraging him to go on.

"Frances, I'm gay. I've been seeing a guy, and we broke up. The stress from the keeping secrets was far too much. I'm sorry I took it out on you."

"You're gay. All right, cool. Want to grab some pizza before it's gone?" I asked, standing up. I knew it was a big deal to him to come out to me—even so, the fact that he was gay wasn't much of a shocker. In the end, he was my brother, and I wanted him to be happy with whomever he pleased. So, if he wanted to be with a guy, who was I to argue?

"That's it? You're all right with all of this?" he asked incredulously.

I grabbed my bag. "You're my brother, Benjamin. Just because you're secretly gay isn't going to change that. Now c'mon, I don't want to miss out on pizza on account of your existential crisis." I held out my hand for him, and he took it.

From there we went to Coney Island, and it was the most fun we'd had in a long time.

***

The tour had started the Monday after the holidays, and it was crazier than ever. Tonight, we were in Seattle—one of four more shows before we went on a break. We had already gone through half of the second leg, and I was shocked by how fast time was going.

I was going over pictures and souvenirs we had picked up in Texas, Utah, and Nevada when we visited there, and I was eating the last of my fudge from San Francisco when I was told it was time to get ready. The boys had already finished practicing and were meeting up with the new band that was going to play the third leg of tour. They were all around my age if not a bit younger. I met up with Everett, who said he wanted to talk. We hadn't done a lot of talking since my confession to him in my apartment, and it was straining on our relationship or whatever we had. I wasn't even sure of what we were anymore. It was bothersome, and I was ready to make amends. I grabbed my coat and an umbrella and waited outside the venue for Everett like he had asked me to. He had to sneak away for a little bit just to get this time in with me, and I was wondering if it was going to be worth it.

When Everett came out, I smiled weakly at him. "Hey."

"Hey," he replied. We were walking aimlessly, and soon enough, our hands slipped into a firm grip, and I knew I couldn't let him go on like this.

"Everett—"

"I know. You don't love me." His short statement made me shrink back inside of myself. "I love you. And I want you to be happy. That's all that matters to me," he continued. He was calmer about it, calmer than I expected him to be, and when I looked up from staring at our feet walking down the damp sidewalk, I smiled at him.

"Thanks. I want you to be happy too, with

someone who can give you what I can't."

"What can you not give me?" he asked.

"My heart," I confessed. We stopped in the middle of an abandoned sidewalk, and the rain was starting to come down.

"Didn't you bring an umbrella?" I asked him, trying to open mine.

"Bea, stay close," he whispered to me, and I looked away from his gaze for a moment and saw exactly what he saw: a masked man carrying a gun headed straight for us. I drew closer to him, and he wrapped an arm protectively around me, putting his own body between me and the gunman as a shield, something I never knew a man would so willingly do for me.

I sensed something in the air that night. It wasn't the rain or the air from the rain, it was something so familiar and yet so foreign. I wanted to say I had been in this exact position before—I couldn't tell you where it was or when. I just wanted to get out of there. I couldn't move or think because everything had happened so fast. I was staring down the barrel of a gun. My heart was pounding in the center of my chest, and I could hear it loudly like a drum in my ears, like Everett's drums. The barrel of the gun moved from my face to Everett's. Then, the gun went off once, twice, thrice—then a fourth and a fifth and a sixth time. Everett was down on the ground, and I was kneeling over him screaming. I thought I was screaming. That's what it felt like. The guy took Everett's wallet and his phone and left me with only a stare. As soon as he was gone, I called for help.

By the time help came, I thought that maybe Everett was too far gone. I rode in the ambulance with him to the hospital, and when the boys got there, all we could do was wait.

The show was supposed to start in thirty minutes. With a drummer down, the other boys were considering canceling the show—canceling the tour if it was bad enough. I was covered in raindrops and in my own tears as Ben tried to comfort me.

"I'll take his place for tonight. You guys shouldn't have to cancel the show when I know all the songs," Splinter said. "Everett taught me some of them. The rest I learned by watching and listening. If I screw up, you can totally fire me, but I want to help you."

For a moment, I didn't even recognize his voice. It sounded so different. Everything was so different. "I'll stay," I whispered to Ben, and only then did he agree to go off to play the show. After the boys left, I looked back to the nurse's station, planning to get some information on Everett.

The nurses in their brightly colored scrubs drove me mad. They were all smiles, rushing about, trying to get everything they needed.

The white walls were dripping with a feeling of false hope and serenity, and the smell of antibacterial soap and saline brought back memories that I wanted to forget. Memories of Mackynsie and memories of the night we said goodbye to our mother when she was admitted into the treatment facility.

I flagged one of the nurses and asked about

Everett. The annoyed look that flashed across her face when I went to the window to ask for information told me I was doing so too frequently. They didn't have any answers for me. They only had answers for his family.

"His family is all the way in New York, I'm all he's got. Please, tell me something!"

The nurse slid a glass door shut to cut me off, and if it weren't for the menacing security guard in the corner, I would have slammed my fist into that glass. Instead I saw my reflection bouncing off the glass, and that's when I realized I was splattered with blood. The EMT hadn't been wiping my face from the tears but had been wiping away blood that had sprayed my porcelain skin.

I rushed back over to my seat to wait all over again. I didn't want to check the time—I was too scared to know how much had passed.

They say no news is good news; I had to believe that meant he would be okay. However, each time the clock ticked in the nearby corner with the wooden carving of Jesus on the cross, I swore I could hear each gunshot replaying in my head. Except it didn't stop after six. It went on for the repeating sixty seconds that passed.

I would hear the doors open and a rush of people enter, and I would hope that it was someone I knew—someone that was here for Everett. It never was.

I had nearly fallen asleep, curled up in the waiting room chair, when I heard someone mention Everett's name. I peered up drowsily and spotted the familiar figure standing at the check-in desk.

"I'm here for Everett Thompson. He's my younger brother."

"Is anyone here with him?" Ryker asked, and when the nurse pointed over to me, Ryker did a double take before turning back to the nurse and in a low, angry tone he chastised her.

"And you didn't let her back. Why? I don't care what hospital policy is! I almost couldn't make it! What if something had happened? At least she was here. Yes, I will fill out this paperwork. Let her back. She's as close to family as he has around here."

When the doors to the ER opened up thanks to one of the nurses at their station, I practically sprinted through. It wasn't hard to find out where Everett had been; I saw a janitor mopping up the blood and another one throwing out bloody sheets.

"He's in the ICU," one of the nurses told me. "Follow the red arrows."

When I found the ICU, I stared around until the on-call nurse asked, "Are you here to visit someone, ma'am?"

I nodded. "Everett Thompson."

She smiled sweetly as if she knew that I needed the smile to get through what I was about to see.

"This way, sweetheart." She grabbed a clipboard and led me through the ICU after being let in with her badge. When I saw him, it took everything in me not to run up to him.

"He's resting, but it isn't really good. Right now, he's as stable as he can be, but we don't know if he'll make it through the night." She told me this in a quiet, calm tone. I wanted to yell and to scream.

"What should I expect?" I didn't look at her, and my voice held no hope. I was numb, and I knew she must have seen it.

"You should prepare for the worst. You should prepare to say goodbye." For once, I didn't care if my tears fell and made my face flushed red with the hot emotion I was feeling.

"Okay, thanks." I didn't know what else to say. What did you say to someone who tells you you're not going to be leaving with one of your best friends?

I walked up to his bed and sat down next to him. I took his hand in mine and felt the coldness in it. I wasn't a praying type of person. I often questioned the worth of prayers in hospitals. Once, I'd heard that prayers in hospitals are more sincere than those in chapels, and suddenly, all I could think of was praying. If hospital rooms could procure a miracle on account of a few prayers, I was willing to shake the dust off my religion and try to make a miracle out of this disaster.

I said a few Hail Mary's, and I said a prayer for Everett and another for the first one to be heard. I was shaking, and I wanted nothing more than for Everett to live through this.

"Hey there, beautiful," Everett's voice said, and when I looked up I saw him awake, trying to fight through the pain. He was paler than usual, almost ghostlike.

"Shhh, don't say anything. Save your energy."

He laughed and squeezed my hand as tightly as he could. "You save it. We both know where this is going."

"If we know where this is going, we can stop it," I said, hope lighting my trembling voice.

"You can only fight Death for so long before He comes to take you, Frances. I'm not going to fight anymore."

I tried not to sob. Even so, my face still contorted in the way it usually did when the unstoppable tears came running out.

"Do one thing for me?" he asked.

I nodded. "Tell me what you need. I'll do it."

"Tell me you love me." My heart dropped into the pit of my stomach. How could I lie to the face of a dying man? How could I lie about the biggest thing before he went into the light?

"I…"

Everett's hand went limp in mine, and the alarms on his machines starting bleeping. There were so many, and I was trying to figure out which one it was coming from.

"Get out of the way, girl! Get her out of here!" The doctors had rushed in, and a nurse was trying to pull me aside.

"No! He can't go! I didn't tell him I love him! I need to tell him I love him!" I was fighting the nurses so hard that I didn't realize Ryker, as well as Ben and the other boys were outside the doors, hearing my every word.

"I need to tell him I love him! That's all he wanted! Let go of me, goddammit!" I screeched at the nurse, and it took Splinter grabbing me to let the nurse guide me away from the scene. Splinter pulled me into a tight hug, and with my face buried in his shirt, I fell into horrible chest-racking sobs.

77

He didn't seem to mind that I was getting his shirt wet or that I was a complete mess. He just held me, and when I heard the doctors calling the time of death, everything stopped. Only, it didn't. It only slowed down.

Ben wrapped an arm around Ryker, who was sobbing. Everett was his only sibling that had hope for a future, and now he was gone.

Rian and Grayson stood in solidarity together, and I was trying to remember how to breathe and how to think. I was unaware of what I was doing, and when Splinter pulled me away from the scene, I tried to collect myself.

We were outside on a balcony, and there was still a hint of rain falling from the darkened skies.

"Do you love him?" Splinter asked after he was tired of the silence.

"I don't know anymore."

"Did he love you?"

"Yeah, he loved me. He loved me for a long time."

"Were you two together?"

"It's complicated." The steady fall of soft rain kept my face damp, and I couldn't tell what was rain and what were tears.

"Bea, if you need anything, I—"

"Just shut up, and tell me about the show. I want to think of something happy. How did it go?"

He told me every little detail of the show. He knew exactly how I needed to hear about it, and with every small detail that he gave me, I felt farther away from the situation I was in.

When we got back to the bus, we were all silent.

We were in our prayer circle stance, except there were no prayers or chanting.

"Everett is gone," Dean started. "It's a great loss, and we will write a formal letter to notify the masses. We have canceled the remaining three shows for this leg, and will continue to cancel shows as we see fit. We're going home, and we're going to take time to mourn.

"Remember, everyone mourns differently. Be kind and courteous, but don't overstep your boundaries. We have therapists who are willing to talk with each and every one of you as soon as you're ready. For now, get some rest. You'll be needing it."

With that said, the tour manager went to his bus, and we all separated for the night.

Everett's death was already trending on Twitter, and I wanted to vomit.

I remembered what it was like to lose Mackynsie. A car accident was quite different than a gunshot wound, but it still hurt the same to the people left behind. You want to do everything in your power to ban alcohol, guns and bullets, and arrest the people who use them. It was never that simple, though. I wanted to scream from the rooftops. I wanted to punch someone in the face. I wanted to *be* punched in the face. I wanted to feel pain and release it—there was an overage of it in my system.

I needed a distraction, so I checked my messages again—and as if on cue, there was an anonymous message.

Anonymous: It isn't what I wanted to do. Now that you've seen what I'm capable of, it's time to pay your dues.

Underneath was a picture of me hovering over Everett, blood and tears on my face. So much blood. I ran to the bathroom, and I did throw up that time.

I was being harassed and stalked, and I didn't know by who or why—and it looked like everything was leading to Crosley. Why would he do this? Why would he go out of his way to stalk me around the United States, send me taunting messages with incriminating photographs, and why did I have "dues," or "debts" to pay? I kept thinking back to what he had said last to me, about our conversation when he saw me before summer started. Nothing came to mind.

I needed sleep, and sleep was evading me. Nightmares kept me up, and cold sweats kept me hot and cold all at once. I couldn't calm down, and when we finally reached New York City again, I hadn't had any real sleep. It was like with Mackynsie's death all over again: the dreams, the night terrors. Everything was coming back full circle—except this time, it was far too much.

When we got home, Ben decided to let us stay in the apartment since it was somewhere familiar. I went straight to my room and locked the door, leaving my baggage in the front entryway and my heart on the floor. I threw myself onto my bed, and all the tears came flooding out. There was no stopping it this time. I couldn't hold back. Everything inside me was screaming for release.

I was beyond hysterical—I was stark raving mad. I rampaged through my room, destroying it, throwing things around and breaking them until I came across one thing I had forgotten about: my songbook. In the midst of all the chaos, writing would help settle me. I picked up a pen I found on the floor and opened the journal. My blood turned to ink, forming words on the pieces of paper that had long since been abandoned.

I sat there for hours, writing song after song. Some were trashy, some were made to be trash, and others made me feel a little less guilty. If I could feel a little less guilt with each song, I knew I'd be okay. I tried writing a new song every hour, hoping that whatever came out would be a form of purging for my heart and my soul.

When I took note of my surroundings again, I discovered the sun had come up, and I smelled food cooking. I came out of my room, and I saw Ben scrolling through his iPad over a plate of food.

"What did you make?" I asked him, and he pushed a plate over to me.

"Sit. I want to talk with you while you eat."

I sat down, contemplating the food on my plate.

"I think it's time for a change of scenery," Ben declared.

"What do you mean?" I asked.

He showed me his iPad screen. He was on some real estate site looking at houses that were near the Dartmouth main campus. The one he showed me was beautiful, and I could imagine living there happily.

"Ben, are you trying to say we're going to

move?"

He brought his iPad back to his lap. "I'm saying *I'm* going to move. You're going to Dartmouth, and I'm coming with you whether you like it or not. I need to watch out for you, and I think New York is done for me."

I smiled and leaned over the table to hug my brother. Out of everything that had happened, this was the best news I had received in a long time.

"I'm going to be making food all day," he said. "Wake up when there's food then go back to sleep. You need sleep, Frances."

I yawned and then nodded. "Yeah, yeah. Okay. I'll go to sleep now." I went over to the couch, pulled an afghan over my body, and positioned myself comfortably to fall asleep.

I dreamed of living near Dartmouth with Ben and never having to worry about losing anyone ever again. I dreamed of how happy we would be.

I woke up to the smell of food again.

"Bea, your phone has been ringing off the hook," Ben told me when he saw me sitting up. "You should probably check it."

I got up groggily and went to go check my phone, and my blood ran cold. More anonymous messages, more threats that were even more taunting. I tried to delete all of them, but they kept coming. One message after the next, they continued to ring in.

"Frances, wake up! Wake up, Frances!" Ben was shaking me awake, and I sat up with a start. Ben's face was creased with worry. I hugged him as tightly as I could.

"Bad dreams again?" he asked.

"Yeah, a lot of bad dreams."

"Well, I've got the cure for that." He handed me a plate with a sandwich and my favorite bag of chips next to it.

I ate slowly in silence, trying to keep my shaking to a minimum. I didn't want to appear too skittish.

When I was done, I went to start cleaning my room from top to bottom until I could find my phone, and when I did, there were no anonymous texts, no threats, and no taunts. There was nothing. I don't think I had ever been so relieved to have nothing on my phone.

When I finished cleaning my room, I put my song journal on my freshly made bed, and I tried to think of something else to write. Before last night, the last song I had written in this particular journal was one I had written with Mackynsie, and it was really all her. I decided to reword it a bit, and revamp it just enough to make it sound like something I'd write. When it was done, I tore it out of the journal, grabbed a match, and lit it aflame. Once it was done burning, I set it in a cup of water, drowning the ashy remains. This was the beginning of a new era for me, and I knew that. I could only wish that it didn't have come about the way that it had. I wanted some peace, and I figured this was going to be the way I get it.

CHAPTER SEVEN

It was odd seeing Everett lowered into the ground just as I had seen Mackynsie. I didn't want it to be real, so I tried to make it something it wasn't. He was sleeping or going on some underground adventure.

No matter how hard I tried, it didn't work. I was still in a state of shock, and I wanted to wake up from it all even though there was nothing that could wake me up.

The anonymous texts had stopped since the last one I received, and I was wondering if it was over. I suspected I was wrong, and I also had a feeling that something worse was about to happen. It's a funny thing, intuition. You never really know you've got it until something bad happens. Everyone thinks you're crazy or insane, but the moment you're right, *you* think you're crazy—*you* think you're insane.

When I got back to the apartment, my life was in boxes. So was Ben's, but he had less to pack. Our mother's things were off to the side, and we were still waiting to find out when she would be released from Lily of the Valley Rehabilitation Facility. It was odd not knowing when or where she would go home to.

"Ben?" I asked quietly after he had made me a cup of coffee.

"Yeah, Frances?"

"Where is Mom gonna go when we leave? What is she going to do when we're gone?" I clutched the hot ceramic mug, and the heat against my palms was comforting.

"I don't know, Frances. I'm sure they'll help her find transitional living."

Transitional living. Another way to say they'd help her find a place so she wasn't homeless. I wanted her to be okay. I wanted everyone to be okay.

"When is our move date?" I asked him.

"August 30th. Just in time for you to start school."

The fall term at Dartmouth began the third Wednesday in September, so I knew I'd have plenty of time to settle in.

"Okay, good. Why don't you let me pick the furniture? You don't have the right kind of taste."

He handed me his iPad, and I started scrolling through Pottery Barn and picked out most of the living room furniture, as well as his bed and mine, adding everything to his virtual shopping cart. I got most of the dining area and the bathrooms done. When I handed it back, he didn't appear as shocked by the price as I was. Then again, money was like paper to him. He had a lot of it.

"Do you want anything to eat?" he asked, tapping away on his tablet.

"Sure, what do we have?"

"I was actually going to order in if that's okay."

"That's fine. You know what I like, so I'm gonna head to my room."

Ben nodded and waved at me as I left. I wanted to hole up in my room for as long as possible without having to come out. I knew it wouldn't be very long, but looking at all the boxes with my life packed into them made me feel empty. I didn't know how to explain the feeling to have it make any sense. Nothing made sense anymore. I felt whole in my emptiness, and I didn't know how that could be. I didn't care about the details anymore; I just wanted to get through this life in one piece. I was a million pieces taped together, trying to pass off as a whole person when I really wasn't. I may have felt whole in my emptiness, but I knew I wasn't. I was broken up inside, like a childhood porcelain doll fallen from the top shelf. So beautiful to look at, even when it was broken into irreparable pieces.

After a while, Ben came in to tell me the food had arrived. I realized then my coffee was cold, and I dumped it out in the kitchen sink and then went to sit at the table to eat my kung-pao chicken. The fortune in my cookie read:

You will find everything you lost in due time.

I called BS on that one. Everything I'd lost was gone forever, and there was no getting it back.

***

A few days after Everett's funeral, the band got back together at their practice space to determine whether or not they should continue the tour. Everyone from the PR sector of the label was against going forward, however, the band members thought it would be an injustice to stop when they were so close to finishing. I could understand that— though, I didn't know how they would do on the road without Everett.

"What about that kid, Splinter?" Grayson suggested. "What if we hired him as a temp drummer for the tour? He knows all the songs, and he played one show already."

PR nearly lost it when they heard that—though, Grayson was only being honest. He was right too; Splinter was a safe bet. So they called him. He was ecstatic and wanted to start right away. PR had a few conditions. They wanted to film a documentary, which was the original plan for this tour, and ultimately Ben had decided against it. They said if they didn't agree to it this time, they weren't going to fund the rest of the tour.

They wanted to record our every thought and our every move. I thought it was sickening. Then I thought, *What if it helps?*

It was frustrating to be filled with something you could barely recognize. I felt like that more and more each day. I wanted to be freed of all of whatever it was that I was feeling, and nothing seemed to work.

After signing the contracts, and Splinter signed on as a temporary drummer, we went out to eat as a band—as a family. We had pizza, and I had a few sips of Ben's beer. He didn't notice, except Splinter did. He didn't say anything, and for that I was thankful.

After Ben and I went home that night, I went straight to sleep only to wake up trembling from another nightmare. Mackynsie's death and Everett's continued to haunt me. When I got up to get a glass of water, I heard Ben talking to someone. It sounded like Ryker, and I tried to keep quiet and to listen at the same time.

"There were more than three shots. It was overkill. The shooter had it out for Everett. This wasn't a chance shooting—this was intentional."

The guy who had shot Everett had taken a photo of me and had sent it to me later. This was my fault; Everett was dead because of me. The memory of staring down the barrel of the gun flashed before my eyes, and the thundering of the gunshots echoed in my ear. I gasped, giving away the fact that I had been eavesdropping. Ben came to check on me, and he helped me to the kitchen while Ryker got me a glass of water.

"Bea, what's the matter?" Ryker asked, setting a glass of water near my hand.

I shook my head, and I couldn't speak. How could he not know what was wrong? How could he not know what was going through my head? Given, I knew he wasn't a mind reader. Despite everything, he knew where I had been when Everett had died and when all of the drama had unfolded. He even knew what had happened with Mackynsie.

I guzzled down the glass of water once my sobs subsided to hiccups.

"Nightmares...flashbacks," I said.

Ryker asked me a bunch of questions, and I nodded yes or shook my head no to each of them. He whispered something to Ben, and I only sipped more water as they talked.

"Bea, I think you have PTSD."

"What? No, I don't. I'm just...I'm just in shock."

"No, you've got Post Traumatic Stress Disorder."

***

It took a while for Ben and Ryker to convince me to see a therapist, but I reluctantly agreed. I saw her the day before we were supposed to leave for the tour. She told me exactly what Ben and Ryker told me—that I had PTSD. I didn't want to believe it, mainly because PTSD was something I thought people who had been in wars or had been assaulted suffered from. I didn't think I had earned the right to say I had been traumatized. I didn't tell the therapist that, and remained quiet while she evaluated me and went over my case.

When we were done, I went back to the apartment to finish packing. I could tell Ben didn't want me to come on the tour this time—except I knew if I didn't, I wouldn't be able to heal. This was my way to do that.

"Frances, I think you should rest a little while longer," Ben said.

"I've had enough rest," I insisted. I kicked a box that I hadn't realized said "fragile" on the side until

I heard something break.

"I'm working through it, Ben. I'm writing songs again, so please just let me do this on my own. Let me come with you, and let me work."

He finally agreed to let me go with him for the last leg, and I was so grateful I started crying again. I dried my tears and forced a smile. "Okay, I'm gonna go finish packing."

When I got back to my room, my phone was buzzing, and I stared at it fearfully. I looked at it carefully. Though there weren't any anonymous texts, there were a bunch of Twitter notifications.

"#RIPEverett" was trending again. I just needed some peace and quiet. I turned off my phone, and when I went to finish packing, I looked toward the window. It was still shut and locked up with the wind chime dangling from the top and the curtains pulled closed. I started to wonder how anyone knew that that was my window escape. Only a few people knew about it, and those few people only knew about it due to personal experience of sneaking through my window before. I went over to the window, opened it up, and sat on the fire escape looking up to the moon.

"Everett, if you can hear me, please let me know who is doing all this. I'm sure you know all of what's going on now, and I'm sorry I didn't tell you. I didn't want you to get hurt. Guess I couldn't prevent that. If you could tell me who is doing this, who is sending those messages and who is threatening me, that'll be great." I sighed, ready to climb back inside. "I'm sorry you didn't get what you wanted." I tried to hold back the tears as I finished my monologue to the moon. "I guess you needed to go." I went back inside and shut and locked the window again.

After changing into my pajamas, I crawled into my bed for the last time knowing that this would be mine. When we left, we were going to throw it out and replace it with a new one, and with that thought in my mind, I fell asleep. I was trying valiantly to fight the nightmares, but I couldn't escape them. One about Mackynsie and one about Everett, and then the next thing I knew, both of them are dying at the same time.

I think the way one dies says a lot about them. A drunk driver sideswiped Mackynsie's car and killed her instantly. Everett was shot to death over something I didn't know was spinning out of control. I wasn't sure what that said about them. All I could think of was how they were both emotionally invested in me, and they both died when I was with them. Mackynsie had died driving me home, sitting right next to me. Everett had died protecting me and because he was in love with me.

Two people I loved had died when they were with me. Thinking of this made me want to curl up and hide away from everyone, including my brother. However, I couldn't possibly hide from everyone for the rest of my life. Was I worth the loss of another life?

Every time I woke up, I felt as if I couldn't breathe—as if the breath from my lungs had been sucked out of me each time I went to sleep. I needed a good night's rest, and it was obvious that wasn't going to happen. I got up, turned on the lamp, and grabbed my journal to write some more.

I wrote until my hand went numb from holding the pen so tightly in my grip and until I was numb on the inside.

When I was done, it was time to get into the bus for the tour. There was a camera crew in the apartment, and they were already asking Ben a bunch of questions. I put on a hoodie over my tee shirt and jeans, pulling the hood over my head as I came out. I didn't want to deal with them right then, and I got my baggage into the bus and boarded before anyone noticed me and started prodding me with questions.

I found my bunk and saw with sadness that Everett's still had his name on it. Thankfully, Splinter still had his own bunk, and I was glad that, even though he was taking Everett's place in the band, he wasn't trying to take his place in our hearts. I crawled into my bunk, exhausted. Soon we'd be in Colorado, then Kansas, then Oklahoma, and then Arkansas. We would be traveling up the center of the United States, and I wouldn't be able to hide the entire time. I needed to breathe, and I needed to sleep.

Simply breathing had gotten harder since Everett had died. I needed to keep my head above water, keep the air in my lungs, and most of all, I needed to keep fighting.

I was the porcelain doll on the top shelf waiting to be played with. I was broken, and I was filled with nothing but dust.

CHAPTER EIGHT

After the show in Oklahoma, I sat in my bunk and journaled everything. It was a great show. The band had had nothing less than great shows. Could they carry on without Everett? Right now, they were doing interviews for the documentary. First Ben was interviewed, then Grayson, then Rian, and then Splinter. I was supposed to be interviewed last, but I hid out until they dragged me out of my bunk. I didn't want to talk on camera about Everett's death or anything else for that matter.

"Frances, it's your turn," Ben called from the other side of the bus. I remained silent. The last thing I wanted was to be recorded as I poured out all my weepy, messy feelings about Everett.

"Frances, c'mon, it's your turn," he said again. I kept drawing and writing, and when he eventually came up to my bunk, I shot him a stare that told him everything he needed to know.

Of course the camera crew was behind him, aiming the cameras at me. I tried to conceal my face with my sketchpad—though, I knew they would still get me on camera even if my face was covered with a large drawing book.

"Not now, guys," he whispered to them. They lowered their cameras—though, I could tell by the red blinking light that it was still recording.

"Frances, what's the matter?"

I shook my head and looked over to the cameras.

"Do you not want to talk to them right now?"

I shook my head. "I don't want to come out right now."

He patted my head gently and went back to the camera people.

"She isn't feeling up to it right now, maybe later." He was pushing them back toward the front of the bus, but I could still see one camera aimed right at me.

Trying my best to keep my head above the water, I felt like it kept coming up every time I took a breath. The current was strong, and the waves moved higher and higher. Every time I started to relax, I was preparing myself to drown underneath the weight of it. I suppose that would classify as depression. However, I wasn't a psychologist with a Master's degree for looking into people's minds and saying, "You're depressed! You're sick in the head!" I was just an eighteen-year-old girl trying to figure out everything as it came to me. I didn't know how to get past that. Growing up was painful and difficult.

Everyone will tell you you're so young or immature or starry-eyed. It'll frustrate you, and it'll infuriate you. It'll make you want to grow up faster. I can tell you that growing up isn't the solution to the problem. It's finding a happy medium between acting your age and acting young, wild, and free. I didn't really know if there was a place in between all of that that I would be comfortable with—though, I was sure I was going to find out. Though I wanted to act the way people expected me to, I also wanted to feel free again. I was trapped and enslaved by the feelings I had boiling up inside my heart. It was so difficult to describe because it could be described any number of ways and still not be fully on point with what I'm feeling.

Having feelings no one seemed to understand was hard. I wish I had someone who understood. Right now, the number of people I trusted was low, and it was dwindling fast. I wasn't as close with Grayson or Rian as I was Everett, and as for Ben, things still weren't where they needed to be. He was more focused on closing on the house near Dartmouth's main campus and finishing this tour than he was about my feelings.

And then there was Splinter. He was different now that he was the band's temp drummer. I don't know why he changed so much, but it was rather annoying. It wasn't that he was being boastful or showing off; it was his attitude toward me that had changed—though, I couldn't put my finger on specifics.

When it was time for dinner, the camera crew went to find their own food, and I came out of my bunk with my journal in my hand. Everyone must have noticed how often I came out with it as if it was another appendage attached to my body. It kind of was at the moment, and I was okay with that. The boys looked worried, though. I figured they knew what K.L. said to me by how they were quietly watching me like a bunch of hawks. They wanted to make sure that I didn't go over to the musical industry dark side. I knew I wouldn't do that to them, and these songs, these writings and drawings, were for me. They weren't something that I had intended to share with anyone else.

"Frances, can I see your journal?" Ben asked.

My first instinct was to tell him no. I wanted to tell him that it was private. I wanted to tell him that he should back off. Yet, I handed it to him and allowed him to read silently through the pages. Some had been stained by food and coffee spills, while others had been blotted from my tears. It was hard trying to eat and watch my brother read through my deepest feelings. There were some things that were written so blatantly in that journal that I didn't want him to know about. I always complained that no one understood me. If I wanted someone to understand me better, I suppose that reading my journal was a pretty quick way to know what I was thinking about all the time.

He read through every page with scribbles of thoughts and feelings I had inside me.

When he was done he tapped his index finger into one of the last pages and said, "This one, this one I want you to record."

I nearly choked on my egg roll.

Ben leaned forward, and everyone was listening now. "I know you've got it in you. So does K.L., but you won't go to him. I know that now. You need to let this out, Frances. Music is more than writing the song and drawing the art to go with it.

It's playing it out, hearing the sounds in your head come to life at your will. You need to do this. If not for yourself, do it for the person you wrote this for." He handed me the journal, and I looked at the song he wanted me to record. It was called "Reagent."

It was about Mackynsie. I guess Ben knew that or he could just tell. Either way, I didn't know if I was ready to record such a big song.

"I'll get some blank sheet music. You write what you want us to do. We'll be your backup band, and you do your own thing. I know you can do this." Ben looked at me with pride and with something else I couldn't recognize. "Are you willing to do this?"

I don't know why, except right when I wanted to say no I said yes instead.

The band was in a flurry, preparing for my first recording session. I wrote the music, and everyone started to practice. I worked on the melody for the lyrics, and I knew that by the time the camera crew came back we would be recording a song.

Ben was right; I could hear it perfectly in my head, and the moment I heard it come to life was exhilarating. When it came time to record, I was able to belt it out as if I was purging. It was a different kind of purging, though. It was one that didn't hurt me so I could feel better.

"These feelings are never-ending.
They haunt me in my sleep.
Your crown has fallen, and you're a royal no more.
Your reign of madness has ended,
but mine now begins.

*These feelings are never-ending,
and you haunt me in my sleep.
Your crown has fallen, and you're nothing now.
Your life has ended but mine has yet to begin."*

***

When I was done recording the song, the camera crew had gotten back from their extended dinner break, and I finally felt that I was comfortable enough to talk to them. I changed into some presentable clothes: a blouse and a pair of shorts. I did my hair and my makeup, and this time I didn't even think of the contacts that sat on the bathroom sink.

I sat down in the lounge while they set up their cameras, and the first question they asked me was, "How did you know Everett?"

I smiled weakly at them and I went on to explain our relationship.

Ben was behind one of the cameramen, watching to make sure I was all right.

"What was your relationship with Everett like?"

I laughed at the question, and rubbed the underside of my nose out of nervousness. "It was complicated. We were very close, too close for comfort. That's the thing, though. We didn't care. We had this...this form of chemistry that was hard to deny. We just clicked."

"Were you in love?"

"No, we were just close as a boy and a girl can be."

I was near tears, so the camera man handed me a

box of tissues. "What was the last thing you said to him?"

I prepared myself for the great lie I was about to give. If I had the chance to document a moment that never happened, a part of me believed that somewhere, somehow it did happen.

"I told him, *I love you.*"

The cameramen were done with their footage of the day and left to go to their van. When I was left alone with Ben, I could see that he had a million questions running through his mind.

"So, you and Everett were close?"

"Yeah, really close."

"How were you so close with him when you barely saw each other?"

He seemed to be asking the question to himself more than he was asking me. I didn't bother answering. I couldn't explain to him that Everett fulfilled the promise my brother never did. He saw me when my brother avoided me. He protected me. He loved me. I couldn't bear to tell Ben that Everett was a surrogate brother. Especially since I had slept with him.

When I didn't answer, he sighed, and I started to sob.

"What's your favorite thing about him?" Ben asked.

"The way he smiled at me and told me I was..." I wanted to say "beautiful"—instead, I cried out into sobs and hiccups.

"Bea, it's okay. You don't have to say anything anymore. I understand."

I knew Ben *didn't* understand. Still, I nodded and

buried my face into his chest and cried.

He held me as I did, and for the first time since I was twelve years old, I felt close to him again. Losing Everett was going to be one of the worst memories I'd ever have, but his death may be the only reason my brother and I could act the way we used to.

The memory of his blood covering me as well as the sound of the gun firing bullets into his body would haunt me forever. That was bad enough, but knowing that I couldn't perform his dying wish left me afraid of what I'd find in the dark. I felt he would always be there waiting patiently for me to tell him how I loved him one last time.

***

The weekend couldn't come fast enough. This weekend, we had break days, and I couldn't be any happier that we were nearly finished with the last leg of tour. Of course, there were plenty of pranks and chaos happening before, during, and after each show, and I knew it was what they would do in any other tour. Just because Everett was gone didn't mean they wouldn't do this. He wouldn't want that.

After recording my song, I felt a little bit differently. In fact, everyone else seemed to feel differently too. Ben wasn't so worried about the house anymore (he got it, though), and Splinter didn't have as much attitude. I was waiting for the final days until I could go home, pack up the rest of my life, and move on to the next phase.

So far, I hadn't received any more anonymous

texts, and I didn't know if I should be worried or relieved, so I was a bit of both.

I wanted to know who was compelled to stalk and terrorize me, and I wanted to know why killing Everett was a necessary tool in their arsenal. I wanted to know a lot of things and hoped I'd find the answers in due time. I needed to sit back and breathe, but breathing was becoming more difficult. I may not have had the same feelings that I did before I recorded the song, but that didn't mean that they had vanished. I wanted to record every song I could in hopes that would get rid of all the feelings.

Once I got used to the camera crew, I allowed them to film me recording songs. It was odd being watched that way. I was so vulnerable when I was belting out the songs I'd written; I was sharing a piece of me that wasn't meant to be shared. It was a hard thing to do, knowing I was being recorded as I laid my bleeding heart and aching soul out on the table. Soon enough, people could watch this from their own homes. I wasn't sure how I felt about it.

"What is it like being the younger sibling to such a big rock star?" the interviewer asked me.

I laughed. "It's really no different. I mean, it can be when we're out in public together. Even these past few months, it hasn't been any different. He's still my brother. The only difference is he plays live shows to real people instead of me and my teddy bears."

It was the truth. I was Eden Sank's first audience member. Now that I wasn't the only one watching their every move, I couldn't help but wonder if there was anyone else who felt as close to them as I did. I know it wasn't the same thing. One thing I knew for sure was that through music anything was possible. You could transcend through time and space and understand an era you never lived through. You could understand someone else's pain and feel liberated because you were no longer alone. That was music. It gave you peace of mind, something other art forms couldn't. Music never dies. Words are never lost. Through music, we could do so much, feel so much. That was why I loved music. Writing and playing it was one thing—to share it with others was a great blessing. I didn't know if I was going to share these pieces of music with other people, but if I did, I knew that they would have peace of mind because somewhere inside of them they felt the same way I do.

"What's one thing you want to accomplish after you finish this tour?" I was asked, and I smiled.

"I want to be the first one in my family to finish college. I'm going to Dartmouth in the fall."

"What are you majoring in?"

"Music."

"Taking notes from your brother?"

"No," I said. "I'm taking notes from myself."

"Okay, that's a wrap for today."

Once the camera crew was done, I went to shower off some of my makeup and hair product, which was way more than I usually wore.

I changed into my pajamas and wrapped my hair in a towel then went around to the lounge to see what was for dinner.

"Chinese," Splinter answered.

"Again?"

"You should know how this band feels about their Chinese food."

I let out a sigh and told him my order since it was his turn to order it. I decided to go with something a bit healthier since I could tell the kung-pao chicken was adding to my waistline. When Splinter was done ordering, he sat down next to me and flipped on the TV.

"Why do you have a towel on your head?" he asked.

I looked at him as if he was crazy. "Don't you do this too? I mean, with your man-bun and everything, surely you know how to towel dry your hair."

He laughed, and so did I. We began shoving each other playfully until we couldn't breathe from the laughter.

"I don't have a man-bun!" he said. Today, his hair was long and flowing majestically.

"Not today," I said. "Except on every other day you have a man-bun."

He frowned, and I sniggered, and when I went to flip the towel off of my head to get the excess water from my hair, he hugged me tightly, causing me to lose the towel and have my wet curly hair stick to him.

"Splinter, what on earth—?"

"You're kind of normal right now, so I thought it would be okay to hug you."

I shoved him off and grabbed the towel. "I am always normal, and it is never okay to hug me. Ever." I ran my fingers through my curls and started to French braid my hair. Splinter was watching me instead of the TV.

"Do you want me to braid your hair too, Splinty-kins?" I asked in a baby voice.

"Sure, why not?"

Once I tied off my braid, I looked at him like he was crazy. "Are you being serious?"

He nodded, and sat in front of me with his back facing me. "Do that braid you did on your hair to mine."

I did as he asked. When we were done laughing from taking all the pictures and posting them to Instagram, the boys came out to see what we had done and laughed along with us.

That was the most any of us had laughed in a long time. It was really the most we had laughed since Everett died. For that, I was grateful. I was glad we were able to laugh again. Although, even though I was laughing on the outside, on the inside, I was still crying into the void.

CHAPTER NINE

The tour was coming to an end, and I was remembering little things we did together when the band was still whole. Like playing Twister on the moving bus as we left Tennessee, shopping in a mall in Minnesota and eventually running away from rabid fans, and watching Rian and Grayson make Vines together that often involved makeup, wigs, and silly sunglasses. My memories were slowly fading, and as the days passed, I wondered if it was possible to make any more memories that didn't have Everett somewhere in them.

It was late when I had gone to bed last night, and I was hoping to at least get an extra hour of sleep.

Much earlier than I had hoped, I felt a nudge.

"Bea, we're here," Ben whispered to me. I woke up and then remembered I wasn't in my bunk. I had fallen asleep in the back room with Ben, and I didn't even care. We were cuddling, which for most siblings would be weird—though for us, it was second nature. I detached myself from him and sat up, running my fingers through my hair. I needed to run a comb through it or use some detangling spray.

The knots in my hair were to die for, and not in a good way.

"Where are we, again?" I asked him.

It was quiet in the bus, and I wondered if we were the only ones up.

"We're in Arkansas. We'll be headed to Little Rock in an hour. You should go shower before everyone else wakes up."

I nodded and did as he'd asked me to do. It was nice of him to offer me the shower first and to wake me up when he did. That way, everyone else could sleep in, and I could take advantage of the shower and all of its mobile glory. Of course, this was before I saw the time. It was four in the morning, and I couldn't believe that I was even awake this early.

I showered and used the last of my detangler in my hair, and then I dried off and went to get dressed. Since I thought everyone was still asleep, I went into the bunker area in my bra and underwear to grab clean clothes. I had grabbed a shirt when I heard a whistle, so I rushed to cover myself and saw Rian poking his head out of his bunk.

"Rian, what are you doing up?" I asked harshly.

"I heard someone in the shower, and it made me need to pee."

He got out of his bunk shirtless and clad in boxers. He slid right past me, our bare skin brushing against one another's for just a brief moment. Rian had the tendency to cross many lines and break every rule; sometimes, I often thought that if I wasn't his bandmate's little sister, he would treat me as a groupie. He treated every pretty girl he saw

106

like a groupie.

After I pulled my shirt over my head and put my hair up in a bun, I slid on a pair of pants. Buttoned and zipped up, I was in the clear; no one else was going to see my pink polka dot bra and matching undies. When Rian was done with the bathroom, I managed to squeeze back in to do my makeup, and when I was done, everyone was waking up and wanting their bathroom privileges.

One of the times Everett and I were left on the bus alone, I had come out of the bathroom right as he was passing by, and we had collided into one another and collapsed onto the floor on top of each other. We laughed and stared into each other's eyes the way lovers do, and I wished I had known then what I know now. It wasn't love; it was affection. A really strong form of affection. I wish I knew what love was and that maybe he could have stuck around long enough to show me. I'm eighteen, though; I have plenty of time to fall in and out of love with people. I didn't know if it was worth the risk.

When everyone was ready, we all decided to get breakfast at a drive-thru. Unfortunately, our bus didn't make the clearance mark for the drive-thru canopy, so we had to pile ourselves inside and order from the front counter. It wasn't normally such a big deal, but with all the cameras following us around and our now easily recognizable faces, people were pouring their hearts out to us about Everett and their love for the band. They asked for pictures and if it was okay for them to ask in the first place. Ben didn't mind, and he took pictures with everyone who asked. So did the rest of the band, including Splinter. For someone who was so bad at social interaction in high school, he acted like a pro when they asked him a million and one questions. I got our food and headed back to the bus, waiting for the boys to join me.

"Frances! Wait up!"

Splinter had just escaped from the crowd that was forming inside.

"Since when did you start calling me 'Frances?'" I asked him, holding the bus door open for him.

"Since it catches your attention more than when I call you 'Bea.'"

We sat in the lounge area and decided against waiting for the others to return so we could eat our food.

"How are you doing?" he asked around a bite of his McMuffin.

"I'm fine, I suppose. How are you?"

"No," he said, "I mean, how are you…how are you with your mourning?"

Ah. He wanted to know about my ever-sinking depression.

"I'm doing better," I lied, and he either couldn't tell or refused to call me out on it.

"Good, I'm glad."

We ate in silence until the boys came back. Then, things got loud. We were all singing and shouting and laughing. It was all about appearances. If I laughed enough, smiled widely enough, and talked happily enough, maybe no one would notice.

***

The show was pretty amazing, and the stakes for the pranks were high. After Ben found a creepy baby doll left on the street, we all took turns and drew on its face to make it even creepier then created it its own Twitter and Instagram account. It was a harmless thing at first, at least until it had more followers than any of us combined. Tour Bus Baby was a hit.

Before we found Tour Bus Baby, I had joined forces with Rian and spiked Ben's shampoo with blue hair dye. Only, Grayson ended up using it instead, and his normally light brown hair came out of the shower in a turquoise shade that made us all roar with laughter.

It seemed like everyone was having a good time, and I was glad. I hadn't had an anonymous text, I hadn't had any nightmares—things were really getting better. When we went back to the bus after cleaning up the confetti, whipped cream, and silly string in the green room, I climbed into my bunk and skillfully changed into my pajamas without doing much moving around. It was something I had mastered during the second leg of the tour.

Usually after shows, the boys wanted to shower, and that could take all night with as much as they sweated during their performances. I eventually got fed up with all the rushing from the bunks to the bathroom and to the lounge, and figured out a way to change without being seen or getting in anyone's way. It was truly an art form.

When I was done and the boys had finished all their bathroom business, I went to brush my teeth for the night. When I was done and I came back, I checked my phone. It was mainly Twitter feed updates and trending hashtags about Eden Sank and Tour Bus Baby. And this message:

Anonymous: Tick, tock. It's like a clock. Pay your dues, or your head will meet with my Glock.

Wide-eyed and terrified, I deleted the message. I tried to hide my trembling by getting under the covers in my bunk and pretending to sleep. I needed to tell someone, but who could I even tell? I knew Splinter knew something was going on even though he hadn't mentioned it.

I found it hard to sleep that night. The last time I had such trouble sleeping on the bus was the first few nights. Everett had told me a trick: "Put in some headphones and listen to a playlist. It'll block out the noise of the bus, and it'll help you asleep."

I put on the 8tracks app and found a playlist. The first song that came on was, "Saturday Smile" by Gin Wigmore.

I fell asleep shortly, and I knew wherever we were headed next, I would be okay for the night. This person, whoever was sending me these texts, was only trying to scare me. I didn't want to admit that it was working, I'd be lying if I said I wasn't a little frightened. However, I had to believe they couldn't hurt me when I was with my brother and his band. I had to believe I was untouchable when I was with them—otherwise, I'd never feel safe. I didn't know how I'd ever feel safe when I was on my own, except I wouldn't be on my own for a while. It could wait. At least that's what I wanted to believe.

The next morning, I woke up to the smell of bacon and eggs. It was enough to get me to crawl out of bed and track down the source. The boys were all sitting around the table, eating, and when I sat down to join them, I noticed how quiet they were being.

"What's going on, guys?" I asked, piling food onto my plate.

"Nothing, Frances," Rian said sharply.

Though curious about what might be happening, I didn't prod any further. I would have to find out like everyone else in the world: through social media. I checked my phone underneath the table, and what I found left me in disbelief. They had found the person who'd shot Everett—and he was dead. Apparently, the guy came forward with some information about another planned shooting, and he couldn't even get through the door of the police station because someone had shot him on the front steps, execution style.

"What does this mean?" I asked quietly.

"We don't know, Frances," Ben said gently. "They're going to investigate, but this isn't our business. It's the business of—"

"Everett's family, I know. But he's our family too!" I cried out.

They had to tell us something. If Ryker could tell Ben that his shooting was intentional, then maybe he could tell us what was going on with the shooter. I wanted to know—no—I *needed* to know. Whoever this guy was, he was going to come after

111

me next. He held the answers to the reason I was being harassed so relentlessly, what my "dues" were, and who I needed to pay them to. Now, he was dead, and someone else held the answers I desperately sought.

Violently shoving my plate away from me, I rushed back to the bunks and curled up into a ball. I didn't know what to do about this. I was only eighteen, and I had the world on my shoulders. That's what it felt like every damned day. The weight of the world was breaking my back, and I had no one to help me take a load off. Everything was falling to pieces when it should have been falling into place, and I didn't know how to ask for help. I was helpless, and I was filled with remorse all over again. I didn't realize I had been crying until Ben squeezed himself into my bunk and held me.

"We were going to wait to tell you," he said, and it only made me cry more.

"You could have at least tried to act normally," I replied through the tears.

"We couldn't. We couldn't be loud and obnoxious with this on our minds. We knew how it would hurt you, and it hurt us. We couldn't bear to do that to you. Sissa, I'm sorry. I'm so, so sorry."

I cried even more. Whenever he called me Sissa, the nickname wrapped a secure layer of love and protection around me. Right then, I felt frayed at the edges and like a piece of junk. But once he called me Sissa, it was as if none of that mattered. It used to annoy the crap out of me, and now that he called me that stupid little name, I was a heaping mess of tears.

"Today is a break day. Why don't we go look around town?" he suggested.

"Where are we?"

"We're in Springfield, Missouri. We can look around if you want. We don't have to do anything drastic. We can wear wigs and costumes to hide from everyone so no one will know that it's us."

"Yeah, okay. Let's do it."

We got dressed in clothes that would easily blend with the crowd, and Ben wore sunglasses and a beanie, as well as a jacket to cover his arms full of tattoos. I dressed in my usual attire of a tank top with an open flannel shirt, denim shorts, and Converse. Today, I had my hair up in a bun, and my eyes were covered by a pair of aviators. When we went out to go sightseeing, it was wonderful. We spent the day eating and doing everything we could within a few hours. When the sun was setting, we went over to a park and looked at the horizon while eating convenience store burritos, something I told Ben we would be paying for later that night.

He wrapped an arm around me. "You know, you're young and wild. At least you can be. Frances, the world is yours for the taking. You can literally do anything you want. I'm not saying that because I'm your big brother and I believe in you more than any college or manager ever will. I say that because it's true.

"You're my little sister, and you've been through so much in such a short time. It's sad, but let me tell you something I learned a long time ago: the people who have seen the most tragedy end up having the most success in life. You know why?"

I shook my head, and he smiled.

"They never give up—that's why. They've been to Hell and back, and they survived. You're a warrior, Frances Beatrice Morrison. You fight to get what you want and what you deserve. You'll do whatever it takes to get on top. I know this since I've done the same thing. We're bred to be fighters, Frances. We weren't born to be quitters. We were born to fight. And fight we will, until our last breath."

I laid my head against his shoulder. It was nice to hear all that from him, and it gave me a bit of hope. Hope for a future I had trouble envisioning at the moment. I knew everything would be all right. As long as I had Ben by my side, I would make it out alive. He was right; we weren't born to quit— we were born to fight. I was being a quitter when I needed to suit up and take back what was mine. I needed to find the warrior within me and let her take over. Everything that was happening to me was for a reason, and I wasn't going to let it take me down now. Not when I had so much to live for.

The world was mine, and I was going to take it.

CHAPTER TEN

Our last day in Missouri went really well. We had another show, and once that was wrapped up, we were on the road again. I kept remembering little things again, things that we had done together during the summer up until Everett had died.

One particular day, Splinter and I were alone on the bus. He was playing Taylor Swift's album *1989*, and I was reading a book. I asked him to turn down the music, and he refused.

"Don't you like T. Swift, Bea? C'mon, she's like a queen," he said, which made me laugh.

"Sounds like you love her."

The song "Shake It Off" came on, and I saw him switch on the repeat button on the sound system.

"I'm gonna play this song until you admit that you like her even just a little bit."

He was dancing to the song, and I was trying to ignore him by shielding my eyes with the book. It was no use. He was being *so* obnoxious.

"Splinter, cut that out. You're being annoying."

"Am I? Good! Come dance with me, Bea." He was doing the Carlton, and all I could do was shake my head.

"I'm not dancing with you." The song played another three times until I finally gave in. I was dancing with Splinter and lip-syncing to the song. It was ridiculous, but I kind of did like Taylor Swift. It was more of a guilty pleasure, though. I remember how freeing it was.

"Bea?" Splinter called out to me.

"Yeah?"

"Are you sure you're okay?" he asked as we drove through the sunset.

"Sure, I'm okay."

I looked at him closely, and I thought how I really had misunderstood him in high school.

"I'm sorry," I blurted out.

He looked at me curiously and asked, "Sorry for what?"

"I'm sorry for being such a bitch in high school. You didn't deserve it."

He laughed.

"That wasn't meant to be funny, Splinter!" I said, slamming him with a pillow.

"I know it isn't. It's just...I never thought you'd be the one to apologize. I guess I was wrong." He shrugged. "I guess you are doing better."

"I guess I am," I answered.

"Okay, kids, time for bed," Ben yelled, and I groaned. I may have been in my pajamas, but that didn't mean I wanted to go to bed right then and there.

"Fine, five more minutes. No more!" He was acting more like the mother we never had as the days passed. It made me want to laugh and cry.

"So, we've got five minutes. What do you want to do?" Splinter asked.

"Relax, I suppose."

He faked a snore, and I glared at him.

"You might as well go to sleep with that attitude, Bea. We need to take advantage of these last five waking minutes!"

"Yeah, you do what you want to do. I'm just going to relax."

He let out a sigh and made his way out of the lounge and back into the bunk area.

While I was relaxing, I tried to think of Everett and Mackynsie. At all I could do was see their deaths: Mackynsie and her car accident and Everett getting shot. That's all I had left of them. I didn't have any pictures of Everett, and all the ones I had of Mackynsie were back at home, packed away in boxes. I wanted a part of them that no one could take away from me, that not even time could take away from me.

Time takes everything away eventually, and someone can always steal your happiness if you let them. I had memories of them stored in a drawer in the back of my brain, but was it really enough to remember them forever? When I first met Mackynsie, we were in kindergarten, and we had been in the middle of a fight with two girls over some crayons. It was ridiculous, but we were ready to tag team those girls together.

After spending time in the corner together, we had promised we would always have each other's back.

"Promise?" I had asked her.

"I promise," she'd replied as we were told not to talk.

From there, it was pure chaos. We always managed to get into some form of trouble, and we moved from corners to detention desks, to after-school punishments. It was always worth it. She always did have my back, and I always had hers. That didn't change until we went to Rosewood.

Things were different between us there, and quickly noticed how different she was. A lot had changed for me too. I wasn't a virgin, and she was, I didn't have a boyfriend and she did. Even though it was petty stuff, we still had plenty of differences that were piled up against us. Despite it all, it was hard to not keep up with one another. She was in charge, and she was the star of the school. I was a nobody.

"Bea, it's time for bed," Splinter called.

"Fine, let's catch some 'z's."

While I was walking back into the bunk area, I wondered idly why Ben wanted us to go to bed so early.

***

The first time I saw Eden Sank play live was in the living room in an old apartment Ben and I lived in with our mother. I was eight years old, and Ben had just turned sixteen. He thought he was all that because he had gotten his driver's license and a beat-up old car that he had been saving up for since he was twelve. It was a rust bucket and a gas-

guzzler, but he loved it. This was also the first time I met the boys. Rian, Grayson, and Everett. They played some song they had been working real hard on, and it wasn't that bad. It wasn't that great either. I had set out all my stuffed animals like they were watching along with me, and when they were done, the boys bowed to us and said, "Goodnight, New York!" as if we were an actual audience. Humble beginnings for these guys and they never let the fame get to their heads. Even the high school popularity crap hadn't affected them. They didn't get big headed over any of it. I appreciated that. It showed me that being humble was the best way to be.

"Wakey, wakey, shake and bakey!"

I heard this being shouted from what must have been a megaphone, and it was almost like my last memory at Rosewood when that asshole of a guy used a megaphone against Splinter.

I jumped out of my bunk and snatched the megaphone from Rian.

"Who made you God and allowed you to use a megaphone this early in the morning? Stop it. Just stop!"

I threw the megaphone off to the side, and went to the bathroom to laughter coming from the bunks of the other band members.

When I was done getting ready, I went into the lounge, where breakfast was waiting. I piled food onto my plate and ate silently until everyone came in from the bunks. Most of the guys were still in their PJs, all except for Ben. Ben was dressed to the nines, and I was wondering what on Earth had made him dress in a fancy shirt and tie.

"That tie clashes with that shirt," I said, hoping to annoy him.

He looked down at his tie and his shirt, and he must have believed me because he muttered something to himself as he rushed back into the bunk area. I snickered.

"Don't get on his nerves today, Frances," Grayson said in his normal soft tone. He had left for a moment, and when he came back he was wearing similar attire as Ben.

"Why are you guys getting so dressed up?" I asked him.

"Today we're meeting with the human resources sector of our label. They say it's really important."

I cringed at the thought. Human Resources was one of the scariest sectors of all the sectors in any company. They could make or break you. I was pretty sure Ben and the boys felt the same way.

Soon enough, they were all showered and groomed and dressed similarly to Ben. When Ben came back, he had a variety of ties and a look of desperation on his face. He looked at me for help.

I picked a better tie and tied it around his neck. "You'll do great," I told him with a smile.

He let out a sigh and nodded. "Okay, I think I'm ready. Bea, why aren't you ready?" he asked, looking at me. I looked at myself and looked back to him with a questioning glance.

"I am ready. Why do you think I'm not ready?"

"You have to see HR too."

I groaned, and rushed back to the bunk area to

choose a nicer more feminine outfit than my skinny jeans, tank top, and nasty flannel shirt. I chose a pair of straight-legged jeans, a nice flowy blouse, and pinned my hair up.

"I wish you would've told me this last night. My hair is horrendous," I said to Ben as he passed by.

"I'm sorry—it wasn't definite until this morning."

He pressed a kiss to my cheek, and I wanted to strangle him. I knew I was going to go off at any minute, but he was being quite charming, which made my raging anger disperse. When I was done "getting ready" again, I went over to the lounge area and found that all the breakfast food was gone. Everyone had eaten, and someone had even stolen food off my plate. This would normally make me angry—though, I decided to let it slide today. Everyone was obviously high on anxiety and stress already.

When we were in the main office of the label that Ben was signed to, we were called back to the HR section of the building. We were led back by a perky blonde who had a knack for showing off the rack God—or rather, a plastic surgeon—had given her. It was obvious that her breasts were bigger than what they were in her employee ID photo that was stuck in her cleavage. She insisted that they were natural after Rian had asked many inappropriate questions. However, looking at her employee ID, I knew better.

She left us seated in a room with a long black conference table with matching leather chairs that swiveled. Ben and I sat next to each other, Splinter sat next to me, and Grayson sat on the other end of Ben, with Rian next to him. I was wondering why we were here or if we were in trouble. I was hoping it wasn't about Everett. My stomach dropped when a bunch of men and women in suits filed in with reams upon reams of paper and clipboards hugged to their chests.

"Welcome, welcome," one bald guy said. I assumed he was the one in charge because he sat at the head of the table. Everyone else flanked to the sides, and we were waiting for them to unload their news onto us.

"So, we're here on behalf of the Thompson family."

My heart sank—this was about Everett.

"They want to know how you plan on using Mr. Thompson's shares into the band now that he has passed. I am aware that you have a temporary drummer—although, he isn't a permanent fix."

I glanced over at Splinter, who looked like a puppy who had been kicked in the side. Ben explained the band's plan for Everett's shares. I was beginning to feel sick, and I needed some air. I was getting hot, and I couldn't breathe. I could feel hands on my shoulders, but heard no voices. My head was between my knees as I tried to catch my breath. I didn't know what happened, at least until Ben explained it to me later that night.

"You had a panic attack, Frances."

"I've never had one before, so why would I have one now?"

While I ate my broccoli and chicken from the nearest Chinese food place we could find, Ben began to explain.

"Things have changed a lot recently. Panic attacks can happen to anyone. Certain things happen, and they become a trigger. When it becomes too much and we aren't paying attention, we have panic attacks. It sucks, but it happens."

"I'm assuming you've had panic attacks by the way you're talking."

"Yeah, I have."

I paused for a moment and looked to my brother with a saddened expression on my face. "When was the last time you had one?" I asked, hoping that I wasn't being too nosey.

"A long, long time ago."

I could tell he was lying.

"Fortune cookie time," he said, changing the subject.

"What does yours say?"

He ate the cookie first then read the fortune aloud.

True love is around the corner.

We laughed, and when I opened mine and ate the cookie, I read mine:

Proceed with caution— someone is out to get you.

Ben laughed at this. All the while, my blood ran cold.

Fortune cookies weren't always accurate. I mean, Ben's said true love was around the corner.

What kind of fortune was that?

When I was getting ready for bed, I found Splinter out in the lounge by himself, drumming his fingers on the table.

"Splinter, you all right?"

"I guess. I guess I got my hopes up."

I sat down next to him. "I think I did too."

I rested my head on his shoulder, and he wrapped an arm around me. If we were still in high school, this would have never happened. I wouldn't have even gone near him. Now that I was no longer in high school and I was college bound, I could see how ridiculous high school really was. All the unwritten rules of high school societal bliss and chaos were all a bunch of BS.

When we went to sleep that night, I could feel a sense of closeness with Splinter, something I'd never imagine myself saying if we had never left Rosewood. It was odd how things work out in the end. People you thought you hated could turn out to be the people you'd need the most. People you thought you loved could bring you down into a dark abyss without any real hope of escaping.

The people you thought loved you did something far worse: they pretended to love you despite all your flaws, and with a beautiful and convincing façade, they'd tell you they had your back.

CHAPTER ELEVEN

"Ben!" I shouted from my bunk.

"What is it, Frances?" he asked, clearly irritated, walking up to my bunk.

"What do you think of this guy?" I asked, showing him a picture of a German model. He gave me a weary look. "Do you think I could win him over?" I asked with an innocent smile.

He shrugged and then whispered, "I think I'm more of his type." He gave me a wink and walked away without another word.

I burst out laughing, feeling slightly better about everything that was going on. It was nice to know the real side of my brother. I could finally tell the difference, and it was amazing that there *was* such a difference. Things were going pretty well; at least, that's what I had everyone thinking. They thought the old Bea was back and that nothing in the world could bring her down. I tried to make this so— except, it wasn't as easy as I had initially hoped. I tried and tried to be happy again, and every time, it felt like I was trying too hard. I guess that's why they call depression the quicksand of mental health.

The more you try to fight it, the further you sink. I sort of felt that way, like I was sinking further into this darkness the more I tried to hide it. It wasn't fair. I wanted to be happy like everyone else.

There had to be more to happiness than people thought. I wasn't sure what else you had to do to say you were truly happy on the inside—though, I figured it was something I would have to figure out for myself. Happiness was a subjective thing. It varied for different people. One person could be happy making a living as an at-home mother for the rest of their days, raising babies and taking care of their home, while others would be happier by themselves for the rest of their life. Happiness was something we all had inside us; we needed to find a way to lasso it in.

***

I heard my name being called faintly from farther down in the bus.

"Coming!" I yelled.

I got up from my bunk in a daze and went to the front of the bus. Ben looked somber, and I wondered what possibly could be bothering him. I sat down next to him, and he showed me a picture from Twitter: a picture of his ex and his new beau.

I wrapped an arm around him. "Ben, you'll find someone better."

I had to believe that my brother would find someone worth sharing his heart with someday soon.

"You really think so?" I nodded sincerely, and he

forced a smile much like mine. Was he doing the same thing I was trying to do? Hide my feelings and put forth a façade that could fool anyone?

"Frances," he asked, "why are you so sad?"

He saw through me—something I hadn't anticipated.

I laughed lightly, trying to keep my voice steady. "I'm not sad," I lied.

"You're a bad liar, Frances."

Though I laughed again, soon tears ran down my face. "I know I am. I only keep hoping no one will notice."

"We need to do something to make you feel better, then."

I wanted to tell Ben nothing in the world could make me feel better.

"Why don't I pay for your first tattoo?" he suggested.

I couldn't think of what I would want as my first tattoo. So what did I do? Scroll through Pinterest for ideas. I found I was particularly attracted to the floral tattoos that were made to be shoulder pieces, and when I showed them to Ben, he approved. I liked one that was a half-sleeve best, but I decided to start out small. We went on Yelp to look for the best tattoo shops around, and when we found one, we went in.

It smelled of sterile air, blood, and ink. Ben appeared to be very comfortable there, which wasn't surprising considering how many tattoos he had. I felt so out of place and nervous. I had never been in a tattoo shop—most of my ear piercings were done in someone's basement.

When I showed the artist what I wanted, he and Ben teamed up to get me to change my mind of having a small tattoo and getting a bigger piece.

When the artist, Joe, finished drawing up the sketch for what was going to be my quarter-sleeve, I was beyond amazed. He placed it on my right arm, and when I looked at it, I fell in love.

I sat down in a chair, and he passed the tattooing needle over my skin for the first time.

"That's what it's going to feel like. You ready to go?" Joe asked. I nodded, and once the ball was rolling—or rather, the tattoo artist was carving a piece of art into the flesh of my arm—I went from nervous and anxiety-ridden to nothing but pure bliss. I was calm, and I was filled with a feeling of happiness.

It took three hours, but when he was done and he had cleaned up my tattoo, I looked at it in the mirror and tears came to my eyes. Peonies symbolized healing and perseverance, and I needed the healing, and the perseverance was something I was hoping to have dwelling within me. Ben took a picture of the tattoo without the blood, and then Joe took a picture of Ben and me standing together, showing off our arm pieces.

Later, when I got on Twitter, I saw that Ben had posted the picture with the caption:

My baby sister got her first tattoo arm piece. #proudpapa

During our dinner break, when the cameras came on again, I explained the little tattoo adventure to

128

them, showing them my freshly unwrapped tattoo.

Splinter came up to see my arm. "Can I get a better look?" he asked. I nodded, pushing back a curl behind my ear. He gently lifted my arm and looked at my tattoo. "It's fitting and very beautiful." He let go of my arm and went into the bunk area without another word. He and his man-bun were just plain weird.

That night, everyone seemed to be doing well, and the adrenaline from my first tattoo was wearing off. If I could, I would have locked the remaining bliss up in a jar and kept it in a safe place so it wouldn't fade so quickly. Unfortunately, things weren't like that.

You couldn't bottle up your emotions and preserve them. You had to remember them and hope that you would (or wouldn't) feel them again one day. I wished I could bottle up the feelings I had when I got my tattoo and stash them away for when I needed them most. Damn, did I wish I could.

The next few days were spent teaching me how to take care of my tattoo while on the road and preparing for the band's hometown show in New York. While everyone else was excited, Splinter was nervous. He was okay when it came to playing all the other shows except to play Madison Square Garden three nights in a row was more daunting to him than traveling across the United States and playing anywhere else. Everyone had a different emotion when it came to coming home and displaying their hard work for everyone to see, love, and judge without abandon. Maybe Splinter had anxiety about that. He wasn't the most popular guy in Brooklyn. Even though we weren't in school anymore, that popularity shouldn't matter. But it really did, to a certain extent.

Studies have shown that people that were unpopular in high school move on to having successful and happy lives, whereas the popular kids often hit rock bottom. I tried not to wonder what that meant for me personally—though deep down inside, I wasn't like all the popular kids even though Splinter would argue the validity of that statement.

That was what was different about him. He would always call me out when I was being a prissy brat or anything unlike myself. I had no idea how he figured he knew so much of what we called 'the real me'. Maybe it was his ability to see the goodness in people. Maybe he saw what was left of the good in me. I hoped he could.

***

When we played the last show before we headed to New York, I felt a sense of pride. My brother's music was doing so well in spite of everything that had happened over the summer. His record sales had skyrocketed, and "Femme Fatale" was going double platinum. I was amazed by not only my brother's talent but by his humble success. No matter how many times I saw him react to the news of something that should have been so mundane to him, he still acted surprised, bewildered, and amazed. Heck, I did too. We would celebrate and go on with the rest of the tour with a feeling of pure joy. At night, we would talk about how different things could be, often left in tears at the thought.

My first semester at Dartmouth was to start the third Wednesday of September. Ben closed on the house, and he was having me pick out color palettes and new furniture. He was doing a few renovations since it was an older farm house (it even had a bright red barn in the back), and he allowed me to make it a Pinterest dream come true. I picked out every little thing, and once he approved, he would send it over to his contractor. I was happy that he held so much faith in my interior design taste— although, I was a bit concerned by his lack of it.

"Frances," he said one night after a show.

"Yeah?"

"When we get back to New York, we'll be packing up the last of your room and making your new one."

He was more excited about this than I was, and maybe that was on account of him refusing to allow me to have any say in what kind of room I could have. It was his special project, and with the way things had been going, I was worried I would end up living in the barn until my room was the way I really wanted it. All he had allowed me to do was pick out a bedroom set. I ended up choosing an off-white upholstered headboard and bed frame and a white dresser and vanity set. He also let me get a desk and said he would take care of the rest.

"What's your favorite color again?" he asked me.

"Just make the room color some soft, subdued

cool color. Like blue, maybe."

I tried not to pester him about my room and all the things he could do to it to make it horrible. I tried to imagine the best room I could ever possibly have. Besides, I wouldn't be living in it for long. I'd be living on campus for the first year of college. When we were supposed to be sleeping, we often talked about how much we had grown while he let me pick out my dorm room decorations and bedding. I knew I had a roommate, and once I corresponded with her, she said she liked everything I had in mind. So far, things were going great.

Which only meant that things would plummet downhill again. Such was my life.

CHAPTER TWELVE

Before we could officially go to New York to finish off the tour with a bang, we were forced to do a few interviews, some for magazines and a few others that would be considered press releases. We also had to travel to the ceremony at Ben's label where they would officially make "Femme Fatale" a double platinum record. We were on what were considered "press days." They were sort of like break days except all we did was pose, smile, and answer everyone's questions. I was afraid someone would bring up Everett's death and my involvement with him—though, Ben reassured me that he wouldn't let anyone ask such questions. All the while, he hounded me with questions like "Do you like this plum shade or this this duvet cover?" (neither of which really caught my eye) and "What the hell am I supposed to do with only peacock feathers as an inspiration?"

I eventually began to ignore him. If he wanted to keep my room a secret, I couldn't help him. Despite that, he spent the majority of our six-hour flight asking me questions about this or that for my room.

He would show me pictures that had been zoomed in to show me the pertinent details without giving away what it was.

"This is supposed to go on your bed," he would say or "this belongs on the floor."

It took a very stern and motherly flight attendant to scare Ben into turning off his phone when we were preparing to land. It made me giggle, and I appreciated Ben's dedication to his project.

As soon as we hit the baggage claim in the airport, I could see a plethora of photographers and fans with their phones out, ready to catch our every move.

I wore sunglasses, which I had figured out helped with the constant flashing from cameras. I had my hair up in braided French twist and a scarf around my neck that was slightly tucked into my moto-jacket. My outfit was simple and comfortable, and when people recognized me as Ben's sister, they wanted as much of me as they wanted of him. Even Splinter got some attention. Despite Ben's pleas, we weren't able to stay long enough to mingle with the fans; we had interviews to get to. The fans left us alone after Ben's manager came in and asked them to disperse. He had to work harder to get the paparazzi to leave, though.

We traveled from the airport to the hotel then had an hour to rest up. After that, the boys had to get ready for interviews. I wasn't going to be a part of them this time. Ben was entirely intent on keeping me out of harm's way, which included the sharp-tongued journalists who wanted to know everything about me in light of Everett's death and the photo surfacing on the internet.

Ben took a shower the moment we entered our adjacent rooms in the hotel, and Splinter went off to take a nap.

I sat and scrolled through Twitter, knowing all too well that our arrival into this metropolitan area was all over the Internet by now. I saw pictures of me hiding my face despite the sunglasses and the large scarf, pictures of my brother trying to keep me safe from the intrusive cameras. Then, something caught my eye. I saw a familiar face in the crowd behind us, and after zooming in, I remembered where I had seen the face in the photograph: it was Crosley's best friend, Kingston.

Kingston had told me on the last day of school he would be traveling before heading off to college. It made sense that all the anonymous texts I had gotten had picture evidence of me doing something the sender thought to be wrong and that the person sending them could very well be Crosley. Within all that swirling mess, I remembered the conversation we'd had before I left for Ben's tour.

I had been at a party, and the conversation with Crosley had been dying down, much like the atmosphere of the little house party in the center of Brooklyn.

"I think we should call it quits. We don't even like each other," I'd said to him.

"I think you owe me, Bea."

"How do I owe you a damned thing, Crosley?" I'd asked, reaching for more punch. Terribly afraid of becoming my mother, I had tried to stay away from the alcohol.

He'd grabbed my wrist as I was grabbing the ladle from the crystalline bowl.

"Crosley, your grip is a little tight." I tried to break free. His grip had only tightened, and when I'd tried to get away, my struggling had only furthered his violence.

"Crosley, what is up with you?" I'd shouted, and then he'd slapped me.

"You owe me, Bea, and you aren't quite finished paying up yet."

He had pulled me toward the bedroom, and I had taken note that the few people left in the party had been ignoring us. I'd feared the worst. Was this what he'd meant? That I was to pay a debt with my unwilling body?

He'd hiked up the skirt my mother had always said was too short. Chills had run down my spine, and a cold numbness had rolled over me. Ultimately, nothing had happened. Yeah, he'd roughed me up pretty bad, but he wasn't in the mood. In fact, his mood had rapidly shifted from anger to lust then despair. Crosley had been on the floor sobbing. I'd tried to console him in hopes that he wouldn't lash out at me again, and he'd only grown increasingly frustrated with me. I'd left the room then the house with him shouting at me the whole way.

"You owe me, Beatrice Morrison! You either pay up, or you'll die wishing you had listened to me when you had the chance!"

When I'd gotten home, my mother had been missing—though, the scent of her alcohol-infused musk lingered. I'd gone to my room, certain that the

136

scene between Crosley and me at the party had been our official breakup. However, when I'd returned to school the following Monday, as soon as I had entered the main hall, Crosley had come up to me with a big sloppy kiss.

He had been affectionate all day, and even though it was obvious I wasn't into it, he'd forced me to pretend I was. That was the whole game. I had to pretend to enjoy the things he did, the things he said, and the fake relationship we put on for everyone to show that we were the big bad bitches of Rosewood. I wondered if this was what Mackynsie had gone through and if this was why she was so different when we reconnected. After being away from one another and going to different schools for a year, I could see how drastically she had changed.

Coming back to the picture on my phone, every little thing made sense. Crosley had money and the means for a hire-to-kill. His family probably had the money to hire multiple hit men and multiple attorneys to cover all the murders up if someone displeased them as much as I apparently had displeased Crosley. I never gave him what he wanted—a consummated relationship. He wanted that part of me so he could say he owned a part of me no one really else had.

Yeah, I'd had sex with boys (and the occasional girl), but none of it meant anything. The only time it had meant anything was when it had been with Everett. I didn't love him—although, the moments we shared were still special to my heart. I missed him every day. A part of me still felt guilty that I couldn't give him the love he deserved when he loved me so recklessly.

Caged up and refusing to experience my emotions, I believed that this was truly the root of my problem. I refused to feel at all; I refused to hurt, to love, to be angered or to be gracious. I refused to let my emotions get the best of me, and it was finally taking its toll.

"Bea, are you ready to go?" Ben called from the hotel bathroom adjoining our two rooms.

"As ready as I'm going to be."

We grabbed our stuff, rounded up everyone else, and headed down to the lobby. We had an escort to and from the location of the interview. This one was for some magazine, and they would be recording parts of it for a YouTube session. Everyone was obsessed with the idea of getting an interview with Eden Sank since their only drummer had been shot to death and since the lead man's little sister was a witness to it all. They wanted to know more about me, more about Everett's last moments and, furthermore, what this meant for the band. Everett had been a drumming prodigy. I doubted they could hire Splinter permanently to take his place, despite how much he favored Everett in the drumming artistry. No one would be stupid enough to let Splinter's talents go unnoticed forever, though. He was the reason the band was still playing shows and the reason the band was still together at this point.

When we got to the magazine headquarters, we were given lanyards with our all-access passes in them. As we went into the main offices, we were told that we were expected to wear them when walking about the main office and other offices surrounding the building. It was the only means we had to get in and out.

As we walked to our ultimate destination, I scanned every corner we passed. Anything could happen at any time. Crosley or his lackey Kingston could be here. While Kingston wasn't as wealthy as Crosley, he still had enough to get him into any place he wanted without being on a list.

That meant he could be here watching me like a hawk, waiting for any sign of me slipping up and being unfaithful to Crosley. Crosley must have still felt that we were together. We'd never slept together, so it had never been official, at least in his eyes. For me, being with him had been pure torture, and the fact that I had put up with him for as long as I had made it official enough. The thing was, Crosley was more than a little crazy. I had always felt he wasn't completely right in the head, and if I was right about this, about all the messages and the stalking, then I had to be right about Crosley from the beginning.

"Frances, c'mon. You're lagging behind." Splinter grabbed my hand and pulled me toward the lounge we were assigned to, and I swore I heard the clicking of a camera. Maybe I was being paranoid.

If I wanted to keep myself from going insane, I had to believe that money couldn't buy anyone's way into this place, and that the clicking of the camera was from one of the magazine photographers. This *was* a magazine office after all. I didn't want to believe any of the things that were happening were actually happening.

My phone buzzed then, a text message. With a gulp, I tapped to open it, revealing a picture of me looking away from the camera lens and Splinter holding my hand.

Anonymous: Didn't think I was going to stay away forever, did you? Looks like you're slipping up, and you're just about past due.

I tried to hide my trembling, my fear. I had to know who was behind this, and I was fairly certain I already did. I took a moment to go get a bottle of water, and that's when I saw him: Kingston.

"Kingston?"

Realizing he had been discovered, he took off. I ran after him, except he was much faster than I. He had gotten a track and field scholarship to Yale on top of a drama scholarship.

I almost caught him, but by the time I reached him he was already out into the main street, blending in with all the pedestrians. My heart pounding, I went back up to the floor where the guys were. They didn't appear to even notice I had left. No one except for me knew about this. This was a burden I had to carry on my own, and before long, I would be well past overdue with my supposed debt that was owed.

When I returned to the interview, everyone was all laughs and giggles. I remained quiet in the background, watching the interview unfold. Ben was amazing, the boys did great, and so did Splinter. For someone who'd had a curveball thrown at them during his internship turned temp drummer-ship, he was handling the fifteen minutes of fame pretty well.

We would be returning to New York after these few press days that remained. I didn't know how or when I'd run into Crosley. I didn't know what he had planned for me if I ran out of time in his mind. I didn't know a damned thing.

CHAPTER THIRTEEN

Press week dragged on and on. Every day, we spent around twelve hours going between interviews and airport terminals. We were being taken all over the place. The only sense of normalcy I really had was when Ben grilled me about my likes and dislikes for his little project. When I was trying to sleep, though I wasn't quite dreaming, I could sometimes hear him on the phone with his contractor, giving them further details they needed to complete his project. Working on making this house our home was really bringing us closer together, and it also proved to be a great distraction. With the sleep I was losing due to constant jet-lag and the never-ending traveling, I was thankful when we were given a full day's rest when we entered New York. It was great to be home, yet at the same time, I knew we had a lot of time dedicated to publicity and interviews. Just a few more days and then we would be done and headed toward Madison Square Garden for the final three shows of this tour.

Ben was happy to be back in New York, and I couldn't help but feel a mixture of anxiety and joy myself. Joy due to being in the place I was lucky enough to call home, and anxiety due to the fact that once news of my return began to spread, Crosley was going to be waiting for me.

Ben decided we should both take a long nap then he and I would go shopping. He wanted to take me to get a few new things for school, as well as a few things for our new home. It was weird saying "our home." Though at the same time, it was so right. I always knew my home was wherever my brother was, and I knew he felt the same about me.

The fact that he was leaving LA, the place he had called home for the past six years, to watch out for me while I went to school made me feel lucky to have the privilege of calling him my big brother. He was uprooting and changing as much of his life as I was. I guess we both needed a new start after this tour ended.

We slept for about three hours, and I would have slept longer if Ben hadn't woken me up. We went through my suitcase and culled all of my old, outdated, and hole-y clothes, bagging them up in hotel trash bags. There were some things I didn't want to part with, things that held special meaning to me. Like the first Eden Sank shirt I'd ever made and the few things I had that matched Mackynsie's wardrobe. I did need to start fresh. I couldn't have matching days with Mackynsie anymore, so I threw out all the mini-skirts, all the shorts, tank tops, blouses, and dresses that she had bought me to match hers. I threw out all the things I had of Everett's which thankfully, Ben never noticed. I threw out the old excess of my past, liberating

143

myself.

When we were done trashing my old clothes, Ben called us a cab and took me on the biggest shopping spree of my life. I got clothes from all the stores' fall collections that were starting to come in. I got new boots and shoes, stuff for my dorm room, and I even got some new makeup and things for my hair.

After we were done with our shopping, we walked down the Manhattan streets with all the bags, scouting cool places to catch a late lunch.

When we finally located a secluded place, we set our bags down, relaxing without the fear of being bothered. The waitress took our drink order then we scanned the menu. It was a nice little café, and I could smell fresh brewing coffee. I wanted to check my phone, except Ben had started a no-phone policy while we were together. I suppose it was a good idea—though, a part of me was itching to see if the news of our arrival had hit the inter-webs and to see if there were any new threatening text messages.

I had to make myself believe things weren't as bad as they seemed. Maybe this was all some sort of hoax. Maybe it was…no, I knew better. There was no amount of self-assured lying that I could come up with in order to convince myself that what was happening wasn't really happening.

"Frances, what are you going to order?"

"I don't know."

Silence fell over us again, and I kept feeling my phone buzzing on the inside of my jean pocket. Ben must have had the same sensation, since his hand instinctively went to pat his pocket only to remember the deal we made.

"I think the grilled chicken sounds good. You still like that, right?" Ben asked.

"Yeah, that does sound good. And yes, I still enjoy grilled chicken."

Ben was always weirded out by the fact I preferred my food grilled over fried, especially with as much we loved junky takeout food. I had always been that way, and I doubted that it was going to change any time soon.

When the waitress came back to take our orders, Ben asked for their garden burger, and I asked for the grilled chicken. After she had left with our orders, I looked at Ben curiously.

"Since when do you eat garden burgers?" I asked with a teasing lilt in my voice.

"Since I decided to eat a little healthier."

I giggled until I felt my phone buzzing again. Ben and I looked at each other—then, we silently agreed to give up the no-phone policy.

Opening every app that had an intimidating amount of notifications, I saw one thing right away—my face was everywhere. The picture that had been leaked was the picture from the night of Everett's death.

"The murderer...took a picture of you..." Ben said quietly.

Soon enough, Ben was in a furious flurry of activity.

"I'm reporting the photo, and I'm calling my manager. This is going to cause a lot of damage."

"Do you think it's my fault?" I asked him.

"Do I think what is your fault?" he asked absently.

I couldn't bear to look at him as our food was placed in front of us. I left his question unanswered. He didn't know every single thing that was happening when I wasn't by his side. He was oblivious.

A better question I should be asking myself is how could I possibly begin to ask for his help.

***

When we got back to the hotel, I tore off all the tags and threw away all the boxes of my new clothes and shoes. I packed them neatly in my suitcase and laid out an outfit for the next day. A pair of ripped, acid-washed jeans, lace-up combat boots, and a black shirt that had something written on it in jagged lettering. I could hear Ben in the other room, shouting on his phone to his manager about making that picture disappear from the Internet. He wanted nothing more than to save me. Although, I also thought that partially he wanted to save himself. How could the band's reputation survive with that picture of Frances Morrison—Ben Morrison's baby sister—covered in Everett's blood with his dying body cradled in her lap?

I had a feeling that if Ben yelled enough in the right pair of ears, someone would figure it out for us.

I went to sleep early that night. I didn't want to deal with this, not on the day that was meant to give us a rest from the pressures of life on the road.

Now that this picture had leaked, there would be more questions to answer, and I didn't know if I could hide in the background for much longer. So I slept. Unfortunately, I couldn't quite find the solace I was looking for. My darkest fears had leached into my dreams, causing me to wake every few hours. I would sit up and stare blankly at the wall in front of me.

***

The next morning came too quickly. We were in such a hurry that I didn't know what was a dream and what was reality. Everything was a blur, and I swore I could hear Everett's voice along with the others, and I chastised myself about how crazy I was becoming. No one with a sound mind heard voices of the deceased. He was gone, and all I had left of him now was his memory, and the last picture of us together that shouldn't have been taken in the first place.

Dressed in the outfit I had laid out last night, I went along on the ride from the hotel to the conference center in a daze. I was empty, numb all over again. I could tell Ben was worried about me, and as much as I wanted to take away his worry and make myself better, there was nothing I could do. There was nothing left for me to do to make this okay. All I could do was leave and put all of this behind me.

The moment we stepped into the conference center for the press release, I felt faint. Splinter helped guide me as we walked to the stage, and I tried my best to stand on my own behind Ben while he gave his speech.

When it came time for questions, I knew the hot topic would be the leaked photo. Surprisingly, it never came up. No one asked, and no one stared at me like I was the cause for anything at all. No one asked for me to speak; no one asked for me to do a thing.

When the press conference was done, we went back to the hotel, ordered dinner, and while Ben and I made the last minute adjustments to the home we were making together, I asked him, "Have you called to check on Mom?" He was quiet for a long moment. "Have you checked on her at all?" I asked when he didn't answer.

After another long pause, I let it go. I didn't understand how he could have so much disregard for her when she needed us the most. We had sent her off to rehab in hopes the doctors and other patients would be enough. Kind of like I hoped she would be enough for me. She never had been, so a selfish part of me had hoped that the doctors and patients wouldn't be enough to soothe her. I knew it was wrong, but it would be a nice slice of karma, so it didn't feel as horrible as it should have.

After tonight, we would be playing the last three shows of this tour. We would then be going our separate ways. Ben and I were headed to New Hampshire, and Grayson would be heading back to Los Angeles with Rian. As for Splinter, I wasn't sure what his post-summer plans were. Nor had I bothered to ask. Maybe I should have considering how much time we were spending together, and how close we had grown since we'd left high school and gone on this tour together.

I texted him, and we met out in the main hallway in our PJs.

"What's wrong, Bea?" he asked.

"Nothing's wrong. I just wanted to ask you some questions." We slid down against the wall, sitting in the hallway.

"Where are you going to go after this all ends?" I asked. "School? Work? Are you traveling? Are you staying here?"

He looked taken aback by my influx of questions, and when I finally took a breath, he asked, "Why are you so panicked about my after-summer plans?"

Swallowing back my initial impulse to be snarky with him, I simply told him the truth in the best way I knew how.

"Splinter, you're the only real friend I've got left. I know I didn't give you the time of day back at Rosewood, it's only now that I realize how stupid that was. I should have paid more attention. While I was busy being a royal and looking down at you, barely acknowledging your existence, you noticed me when I couldn't even look you straight in the face. I want to know what you're doing because I don't want this to be the end of our friendship. I want to keep in touch. I want to be your friend for as long as you can put up with me, and—"

He placed his hand over mine, cupping it in a gentle grip. "We're going to stay friends after this, Bea. You know too much, and I know too much. We either stay friends or die trying to ruin the other's reputation."

We laughed together, and he gave me the biggest promise anyone could ever give me—a pinky promise that meant we would keep in touch, no matter where we were or what we were doing.

I went back to bed. After tonight, everything was going to change for me. Whether it was good or bad, I wanted to feel every part of it: the joy, the pain, and even the sorrow. I didn't want to repress a single thing anymore. I wanted it all, and I wanted it right then.

Right as I was ready to fall asleep for the night, my phone buzzed on the nightstand. Without a second thought, I checked it. Two text messages came onto the screen display: one from Splinter and one from the anonymous messenger.

Splinter: *These last three nights are going to be the best ever. Get some rest, because we're not going to get much after tonight.*

I smiled at his heartfelt message, and when I looked to the message from my anonymous stalker, I knew that this wasn't going to be an easy getaway.

Anonymous: *Welcome home, B. Pay your debt or live eternally in regret.*

My time was running out, and so were my options. I could only hide from him for so long, and I didn't where I would be safe. Should I ask for help? Should I figure this out on my own? Was I even safe to begin with? I know I didn't feel safe with the threatening text messages I had received nor the stalking. There was no escape.

CHAPTER FOURTEEN

We woke up incredibly early the next morning. We still had a lot to do even though our press days were over. It was the first night at Madison Square Garden, and the boys decided to go and practice there early. This meant waking up at five in the morning and going over to the venue while the production crew and all the people involved in making Eden Sank's concerts a reality were still setting up the stage for the show.

They went into the back of the green room and tried to practice there, and I could tell Splinter was nervous. He was off, and Splinter was *never* off. The poor guy kept dropping his drumsticks like a baby who was learning to grasp objects for the first time. He was *Splinter Nightingale* for Christ's sake. I couldn't believe that he was letting all of this get to him.

"I think it's time for a break, guys. What do you think?" I said. I needed a moment alone with Splinter, and this would be my only chance of getting him back to where he needed to be. The boys all filed back to the stage to see how the production team was doing, and when Splinter stood to join them, I grabbed his shoulder.

"What is it, Bea?"

"Stay here with me; we're going to practice some more." I handed him his drum pad, and he looked at me as if I was crazy.

"I thought you wanted us to take a break?"

"I did," I said. "But you are overthinking everything and ruining yourself."

"Bea, I think you're overreacting."

"Am I?" I asked with a hint of knowing in my voice.

He stared at me with a dumbfounded look.

"They're intimidating you, and this venue is intimidating you. You're off your game, Splinter. You aren't in the zone."

"What zone?"

"Your *zone*. Whenever you play, you go to this place that makes it hard for you to be distracted by the things around you. You're not there right now. You need to find that place again."

Splinter looked at me curiously. "You haven't been ignoring my existence after all." He smirked and I swatted the side of his arm.

"Shut up, and sit your ass down. We're going to practice until you get into that zone of yours."

We practiced and practiced, and I sometimes yelled at him as if I was a person in the crowd trying to throw him off. I threw things at him, and he blocked them with his drumstick, all the while maintaining his rhythm and beat. I was proud when we were done, and when the boys came back from their break, Splinter was on point.

I kept checking my phone. It was filled with notifications about tonight's show. Thankfully, there was no more talk about the leaked photo. For that, I was grateful.

However, there was an underlying feeling I had. I didn't know how to explain it except every time I had my phone in my hand I had a feeling of impending doom, like everything was going to fall apart. Maybe I was being paranoid. Whether it was a feeling, a vivid dream or a vision—some people just knew something was going to happen before it did. They had warning signs and signals that led them to believe they were in the wrong place, the wrong time. I wanted to believe I had that, at least with the feelings I had.

I knew in my heart before it happened…when Mackynsie died. I didn't need the doctors to break it to me or for anyone to tell me a thing at all. I knew as we reached the hospital; I knew the moment the car collided with hers. I knew the moment I woke up and she didn't. I knew, and I don't know how I did. Intuition was a funny and cruel thing to have.

I was hoping that this feeling in my heart was wrong.

***

While we waited for the venue to open the doors, we formed our prayer circle. It was weird without Everett here, and despite how many times we had done the prayer circle without him, it was still an unsettling feeling. Even if it was going to be short-lived that Splinter was a part of the band, I tried to put my thoughts of Everett behind me. A part of me wanted to believe he was sick at home, wishing he were here with us as much as I wished he was. I wanted him back so badly. All these thoughts came to me while we were praying.

When we heard the venue filling up our, energy got higher, and our excitement grew with each passing moment. This was going to be an amazing show; I could tell by the way the boys were acting and how they reacted to seeing the sold-out crowd from behind the stage. I was happy for them—I really was.

From the moment they rushed on stage to the moment they came back for intermission while another band went on, I was in pure disbelief. They were living their dream, and so was Splinter. He wasn't nervous anymore, and I could tell by the huge smile on his face. He was covered in a layer of sweat, and he was breathing heavily, but he was happy. The anxiety he'd experienced earlier was gone.

He came up to me, hugged me tightly, and whispered into my ear, "Thank you."

When they went back on stage, I was a bit distracted. I kept thinking of the last time I had seen Ben before he became as famous as he was now.

It had been the night leading up to Christmas Eve. We had stayed up late talking—though when I had gone to sleep, I had been woken up by the sounds of loud shuffling in the hallway. Afraid that Ben and my mother had been fighting, I'd opened up my door a crack to see outside. Instead of a brawl, I had seen Ben with a backpack on his back, trying to lug a huge suitcase and two different duffle bags over his shoulders.

"Ben, what are you doing?" I had opened the door all the way and had gotten a good look at my not-so-sneaky brother.

"Bea, go back to bed. I don't want to risk Mom—"

"Where are you going with all those bags?" I'd taken a closer look and seen he was holding what looked like a boarding pass. "Are you leaving me? It's—"

"Bea, I'm sorry. I'm doing this for you. I'm doing this for us." He'd pulled me into a tight hug, and I'd yanked a handful of his hair. It had been longer than usual, so there had been a lot to grab.

"Bea don't! That hurts. You can't keep me here."

I'd watched him with teary eyes. "What about me? What about Mom? How am I—?"

"I've got it all taken care of. Here, take this." He had handed me a large brown envelope. It had felt weighted as if there were multiple things inside, definitely more than paper.

"I need you to keep this away from Mom. It's for you and everything you'll need. I'll send more in time."

"Ben, please, don't leave me."

"Bea, you'll thank me one day for this."

I had shaken my head, tears brimming in my eyes. "I'll never thank you for this. If you leave me now, you—"

"You say this because you'll miss me. We will

still talk, I promise."

"If you're going to promise me anything, promise me—"

He'd set down his bags and pulled me close again. Then sang:

> *"From me to you, I'll always be true,*
> *A promise I'll make, one I'll never break.*
> *Together or apart, you'll always have my heart.*
> *One promise I ask of you,*
> *is that you always stay true,*
> *and to keep the faith.*
> *With this, you'll be okay."*

By then, we had both been crying. Ben had hugged me one more time until we had seen colored lights flashing into the living room from outside the window.

"That's my signal; I've got to go."

I'd held onto him for as long as I could. I hadn't known where he was going or when he would be back. I had felt like this was our final moment to say anything and everything to each other.

"I love you, Sissa."

With tears streaming down my face and leaving stains on his shirt, I had said, "I love you too, jerk face."

***

Now, I was happy to be with my brother in a place like this. He was right—I was thankful that he'd left and done all of this for me. If it weren't for all the money he had made doing this, I would have never survived. There was no other way around it. Yeah, living alone with my mother was Hell, which was why I'd usually stayed with Mackynsie's family, the Campbells. They hadn't minded—they'd seen me as another daughter. They'd treated me that way too.

I never did really get to see or talk to Ben after he'd left, so technically our promise had been broken. I eventually figured out where he had been living, thanks to the return address and the postmark on the envelopes filled with money he had always sent me. Eventually, he started to wire me the money through Western Union, so I couldn't see his address anymore. The most I saw of him was the appearances on TV or on YouTube.

I was angry for a while since he did break his promise to me, as well as the fact that whenever he had a show in town he never came to see me. I never did ask him why that was even though I probably should have by now. However, the more time I spent with him this summer, the less it mattered to me.

As Ben and the boys went back on stage for the rest of their show, I smiled to myself and checked my phone again. There was nothing from my unknown stalker. Even if it was still an unknown person, I kept feeling like it was Crosley. I had no real proof other than Kingston being in the magazine office the same day I was and the way he reacted to me noticing him. It was all too coincidental to not make sense. Though everything was leading me back to Crosley as the culprit, I had to have more proof. Though I had a feeling that the proof I needed was the very thing that was going to get me what I had been threatened with: a six-foot hole in the ground.

CHAPTER FIFTEEN

The moment the show ended on the first night, we were all high from an adrenaline rush. It was amazing, and I couldn't believe how far we had all come in three months. Heck, looking back at some of Eden Sank's earlier works, I couldn't believe how far they'd come in the past six years.

We tried not to party too hard when we got back to the hotel, but our excitement and our high energy weren't going to let us back down so easily. Musicians weren't morning people anyways.

The boys rested up while I cleaned up as much as I could so as not to piss off the cleaning staff. When I was done, I went to go take a shower and get dressed. By then, the boys were up and wanted breakfast. The hotel had stopped serving breakfast an hour before they woke up, so after much discussion, we decided to take a trip to a nearby pancake house.

The buzz from people seeing the bus with Eden Sank's logo alone was immense, and I was in a state of disbelief again when I saw how many people wanted the attention of the band members, even

Splinter.

I sat back and let everything happen, which seemed to work in my favor. No one wanted to know me right then—though, I managed to photo-bomb a few of their pictures.

I couldn't believe how loved they were. It made me appreciate them even more because I had loved them first.

I still remember the first time I had met all the boys, Everett included. I was six years old when the band first took its earliest form. One of Ben's friend's had given him an old guitar a few years back, and he would mimic the movements of guitar players he watched on MTV. Grayson and Rian were his best friends from school, but Everett was new. He was the last to join the band, and he was one of the youngest out of the group. Yet he always left an impression that he was wise and not of this time. Sometimes he acted plain stupid like every other teenage boy—though, there were many times I could tell he was an old soul. Despite being new to the group, he fit right in. Somewhere in between all that, he found his way into my heart. I wasn't sure how it started except that one night while the boys were in New York, he decided to visit me. He was mad because my brother hadn't called or come to see me himself. We sat up late eating popcorn and watching old horror flicks. Ben never knew, and I told Everett it was our little secret as I snuck him out the window when we heard my mother waking up.

The next time he visited me, I was fourteen, and I

was beginning to fill out thanks to hormones and puberty. We did the same we had done the last time he visited: watched TV and ate junk food. We stayed up talking again until Mackynsie called me late that night, asking if she could come over. I said goodbye to Everett that night and didn't see him again until I was sixteen. He was visiting New York early in anticipation of the start of his tour with Eden Sank, and he ended up staying at my apartment for most of his stay. That was how we realized we were more than friends. I enjoyed his visits so much and having him so close by. If Mackynsie, who was jealous that I even had had sex to begin with, hadn't caught us, more would have happened. A lot more would have happened.

After that, I never saw him again until he was outside my apartment in Old Trusty, waiting for me to graduate. He looked so happy.

Thinking of this brought tears to my eyes, and by the time the boys were done, we all went straight to our table and ordered our food.

While the boys were talking candidly about that night's show, Splinter must've noticed my tear-stained cheeks. I assumed that to be true once he placed a hand over mine and asked quietly, "Are you all right?"

I nodded and shoved away his hand, continuing to ignore him. I didn't want to tell him why I had been crying, nor why I wanted to ignore him so badly. He couldn't possibly understand.

While we were paying the bill, I brought up something with my brother.

"Ben, we still need to go by the old apartment to pick up the rest of my things."

Ben swallowed down the last of his orange juice and gave me a quick nod.

"If you want, I can drop you off before we do sound check and have someone pick you up when you're done."

"Yeah, sure." Nothing bad could possibly happen while I was packing away my things.

Right?

***

When we went back to the hotel before sound check, I left my phone at the hotel. Who needed their phone while packing their life away? I could use the landline when I was done.

I found Ben trying to do his hair, and out of frustration, he allowed me to help him.

"The landline is still in service, right?"

"Yeah, it is. I get a bill for it every month..." Ben went off on a tangent, discussing how ridiculous it was that he got a bill for it every month mostly due to the fact that he never cut it off and wasn't actually using it.

"I told you that you should have shut it off when you two left," Grayson chimed in when Ben continued on with his rant.

"Yeah, Ben, why didn't you?" I asked out of curiosity.

He shrugged and said, "To be honest, I don't know."

When it came time to get ready for the show, I

dressed in dark-washed skinny jeans and a white sleeveless blouse with an open back. My boots were laced up over my jeans, and I was ready to go back to the place I was leaving behind.

Ben dropped me off, and I hugged him. "I love you," I said. Something I hadn't told him in a while.

"I love you too, Frances. Take as much time as you need. It's not like it's our last show or anything."

I laughed at his comment as I got into his rental car and headed toward the apartment.

Inside, it was cold and stale as if the time that had passed since anyone had inhabited it had taken a toll on it. It seemed dreary, and I could feel the sadness of the apartment swell within me. I grabbed the group of folded packing boxes from the doorway and went straight to my room. I was ready to pack up the last remnants of my life here and leave this poor, sad apartment forever. Though I wouldn't miss it, I couldn't help but wonder if it would miss me.

I found pictures from my childhood, ones of me with Ben, and a few more of me with Mackynsie. Something that was very little known to the fans of Eden Sank was that Ben had taken up photography while I was growing up. After a certain age, there were no pictures of us together since he was always behind the camera. That's why there were so many of me and Mackynsie and me and other friends, and very few of Ben and me. I sat and looked through the photos for what must have been hours before I packed them with care, putting them in a box labeled *"photos."* I found some photos of me and the few people I had "dated" over my high school career and pictures from all four homecomings and one prom. I found pictures from the time Mackynsie and I went skinny dipping in the Hudson River in the dead of night, and pictures of parties we had attended. One picture had Mackynsie with her arms wrapped around my neck tightly, and we were laughing with bottles of Heineken in our hands. I'd almost forgotten about the picture, and I couldn't quite remember who had taken it. It was the summer of our sophomore year. I smiled at the memories it brought back, crying at the same time.

I was officially an emotional wreck. Without Mackynsie and Everett, I was lost. I was going on with my life without them, and it could kill me if I allowed it to. With the depression and anxiety alone, I thought I should have been the one who was dead.

Consciously pushing these ideas out of my head, it discovered hours had passed again, and I'd packed more than I realized I even owned. I'd never get to Ben's show on time.

After making sure everything was properly labeled and stacked neatly, I used the landline to call the venue. I asked for Ben, and was told he was in sound check. I checked the time; it was time for the doors to open. I then asked for Ben's manager, and when he was put on the phone, I relayed the message to him.

"Dean, I'm ready to be picked up." As I said this I felt a strange chilled-to-the-bone feeling come over me. I looked around, and I found that there was nothing to be fearful of.

"I don't know how quickly I can get there," Dean said.

"Just hurry," I said in a low tone of voice. "Please."

"Is everything okay, Frances?"

I bit my lip. "Yeah, I think so. This place is giving me the creeps."

I thought I heard the sound of a camera clicking when I hung up the phone, and then I saw the door was ajar, which left me in a panic. I went to go shut it and lock it until I was ready to leave, and that's when I felt the end of something cold and hard touch the back of my head, right above my ear.

"I've missed you, my precious Bea."

I heard what sounded like the cocking of a gun, and I swallowed a large lump in my throat.

"We're going to play a little game." It was Crosley's voice—there was no denying it.

"What game do you want to play?" I managed to say.

"We're going to play one of my own creation. You want to hear the rules?"

"S-sure."

He laughed in a dark, maniacal way, grabbed my shoulder, and led me to the bedroom.

"This is how we play. Either you do as I say and do whatever I want you to do, or you get a bullet in your brain."

This was no game. This was life or death.

Of course, I didn't really have a choice. I think at this point, I never really did.

CHAPTER SIXTEEN

All of my worst nightmares were combined into one person: Crosley. My fears coalesced into this one moment with him forcing me to do whatever he wished. The gun wasn't against my skull anymore—though, he kept it pointed directly at me at all times as if to remind me that if I didn't play along I wouldn't live to see my brother play his biggest show yet. Waving the gun at me, he forced me to sit on the bed.

"Remember, Bea, you have a debt to pay. If you don't, you'll never see the light of day again," he whispered, pressing the gun to his lips.

"Why are you doing this?" I asked him to the sound of jeans unzipping

"Being as how you're my queen, you've got a duty to your king." He had to be delusional, and yet the only thing I could think of was how he was able to take off his pants so skillfully with just one hand. I had to figure out a way to stall, but he was grabbing my hand and putting it over his groin—something I didn't want to touch. Bile rushed up my throat as he guided my hand the way he liked it.

Soon, I felt his member lengthening, and I tried to keep my lunch down.

"Crosley, I'm not your queen," I said, attempting to make myself sound confident and stern, not so scared and squeamish.

"Oh, yes, you are. Just like Mackynsie was."

Mackynsie! She was exactly what I needed to use in order to stall for time.

"Was Mackynsie a good queen?" His hand movements stopped, and he flung my hand aside.

"Bea, you killed my mood. How can I possibly talk to you about Mackynsie? Ah, well I suppose you should know the truth."

I was desperate, anything to stall for time!

"You see, I wasn't always king, Bea. Hard to believe, right? Mackynsie wasn't always queen either."

I tried to act as if I was really listening except I was actually plotting my escape in the back of my head. I had no clue what I was going to do or how I was going to pull it off.

"When the seniors graduated our sophomore year, Mackynsie was elected queen. Me? I was elected a man in waiting. I was third in line! It was ridiculous, and so was the reigning king. I decided to usurp him."

"Tell me how you usurped him," I said.

"Well, it was Splint-ass. He had been a year ahead of us. I don't know why he was held back. All I knew was that he was next in line from the senior class. I don't even know how he managed to get next in line. I mean, he's *such* a *loser*. Anyways, I took him to the battle. Our challenge was to answer five questions. I already knew all of them, since the last reigning king was an airhead, and I had persuaded him to let me in on them in case this was to happen. I mean it's good to be prepared.

"Anyways, Splint-ass knew none of them. He was silent as a mouse, so I won. Things between a king and queen were different before we were crowned."

"How so?" I asked, my mind racing. Splinter was supposed to be king? Splinter was the next in line? Splinter was a year behind? Apparently I knew less about him than I had previously thought.

"Ah, well you see, the previous kings and queens were never in any real relationship. I wanted it to be different. I wanted it to be *real*. My first order as king was to declare Splint-ass a commoner for the rest of his stay at Rosewood. The moment I was alone with Mackynsie, I told her the rest of my plans."

"What were the rest of your plans?" *Stall*. I just needed to stall a little longer.

"Well, first off, we needed to consummate our relationship as soon as possible. In the way the real royals used to."

Yeck.

"Secondly, I wanted to change the way the whole hierarchy worked. I wanted to change the system to *my* system. I wanted every royal after us to be like this. I wanted it done—except no one would listen. Mackynsie was a horrible queen, and all the queens that were treacherous in the past toward their kings, much like Anne Boleyn for example, were beheaded."

I tried not to cringe.

"She needed a fair trial, though. So I purchased this little guy." He waved his gun around to show me what he had meant. "And before you came along, I used it very much like I am now." He pointed it directly between my brows, and with a smug smirk on his face, he said, "I used it as a tool of persuasion. Either confess to your crimes and do your time, or you die." He laughed and lowered the gun again.

"It's so simple, yet very few listen. It took a bit, but Mackynsie finally listened. I think she didn't want a blemish on her person at her funeral." He laughed again, and this time, he was bellowing from the comment he had made.

"And yet, there's quite a bit of irony in that. Did you see her before they did the closed casket at her funeral? She was a mess! She was hideous as hell. That drunk driver did a number on her face."

I wanted nothing more than to punch him, but suddenly his libido seemed to increase, and he was pushing me back on the bed, grinding against me. There was nothing I could do except block it out. I stared up at the blank ceiling, and after a few minutes, I heard the phone ringing in the kitchen. I was running out of time, but at least someone was wondering what I was doing. The answering machine picked up the call, and I heard Ben's voice.

"Hey, sis. Sorry, I'm running late. When I was on break from sound-check, I was told you needed to be picked up. I'm done now; they should be opening the doors soon. I'm almost at the apartment. I'll come up and help you with the

boxes."

BEEP!

I couldn't hold it in anymore. I screamed. Crosley slapped me across the face hard enough to stun me into silence. He roughly yanked off my jeans, and soon enough, his hands were traveling underneath my shirt.

"Nice tattoo, Bea. It's so damned sexy." He hiked my shirt up, revealing every inch of skin to him. I tried to hold in my disgust, my pain, my sorrow. He assumed I had given in. I thought of Mackynsie and how she told me she had been going to confession a lot since she started her junior year. I never questioned it; I knew she would randomly go when she was feeling guilty of something.

"Bea, I can't get enough of you." He unhooked my bra. "You have been very bad, little girl." One hook unclasped. "I think it's time you confess your crimes, my queen."

He held the gun at my head, and the second hook of my bra was unhooked.

"Forgive me, Father..." I said.

He seemed to be getting off to the fact I was pretending that I was in confession. He didn't bother hiding his smug face and attitude either. He paused from unhooking my bra and lowered the gun away from my head.

My senses were going into fight or flight. This was it. Everything was sharper—everything was louder and more in tune. I could hear the front door opening; Crosley didn't appear to notice.

"Frances! Where are you?" Ben shouted.

This was it. This was my chance.

"For I have sinned!" I said with a battle cry, and I punched him as hard as I could. He faltered, and it was enough for me to push him off. I grabbed my pants and ran toward my brother.

"Frances, what's going on? Why are you—?"

"We don't have time—just run with me!" I grabbed his hand right as Crosley appeared and snatched me away from Ben, locking his arm against my neck, choking me.

I couldn't stand the pain on Ben's face, or how it had made Crosley laugh joyously.

"Did you really think you could pull that stunt and get away with it, Bea?" he crowed. "Did you really think your brother could save you?" He pointed the gun at Ben and tightened his grip on my neck. "We're going to play a new game. You can join in, Benjamin. Here's how it works: Bea, you get to decide who lives and who dies. Either you let your brother die and save your own life, or you let your brother live, and I can shoot your brains against the walls."

Ben was clearly furious—furious and terrified. He didn't know what to do. He'd probably left his phone in the car, and even if it was on him, he couldn't use it right then.

We were both helpless. I looked at him, and I tried to convey a message that could tell him how much I loved him.

Crosley let his grip loosen on my neck so I could speak, and I coughed as air finally returned to my lungs.

"So, Bea. What's it going to be? Your precious brother or you?"

I could tell Ben was ready to beg for me to let him die. I was sure he could see the rebellion and defiance in my eyes.

"Frances—don't do this."

"Ben, make me a promise."

There was silence and tears shared between us both.

"What am I promising?"

Silence came over us again, and without an actual verbal promise to be made, he knew exactly what I wanted. Our little poem of hope.

"Say it with me," I told him. And we did.

"From me to you, I'll always be true. A promise I'll make, one I'll never break. Together or apart, you'll always have my heart. One promise I ask of you, is that you always stay true, and to keep the faith. With this, you'll be okay."

Crosley gagged mockingly. "Are you two incestuous lovebirds done? I have business to take care of, and Bea needs to make a choice."

While I was certain Ben was hoping it would be him I chose to die, I couldn't let him offer his own life to save mine. I couldn't do that to him. I tried to imagine a world without Ben. It would be as if the sun had suddenly stopped shining. It would be dark and cold, and terrible things would follow. Not just for me but for everyone who had ever loved him. My decision was clear.

"Take me, and leave Ben," I said confidently.

"Frances, no!" Ben cried out, and once again, the gun was pointed right behind my ear.

"Any last words, Bea?" Crosley taunted.

I didn't have enough time for the speech I had wished I could give him—though, I knew what would be enough in its place. "I love you, Ben."

Tears streamed down my face, and with the sound of a pop, and instantaneous pain, I fell slowly to the ground. Everything around me was in slow motion. I could still hear, which was weird. I thought that maybe it was an effect of the afterlife coming for me. Maybe I was in the in-between, waiting to find out where I would go.

I could hear the sounds of fighting, and another bang. Someone dropped to the floor next to me, and I couldn't tell who it was. My vision was blurry...I was sure it was going to go next. Then I heard Ben's voice, and he was talking to me while he was talking to someone else.

"Brenna—Brenna stay with me."

Who is Brenna?

"Frances, please hold on. Stay with me!" His warm hand grabbed mine, which was slowly growing cold and losing all feeling. "Please hurry! He shot her in the side of the head. I shot him with his gun. God, what has happened? Please help me! I can't lose her. I can't! Brenna, stay with me. Please don't let this be our final show."

Brenna was the girl my mother always thought I was in her delusional state, so why was he confusing me with her? Maybe I was delusional, or he was in shock; perhaps that was how he was reacting to it.

I wouldn't know, because soon enough everything faded into darkness.

CHAPTER SEVENTEEN

Despite being raised Catholic and taught otherwise, I had never really believed there was an afterlife. I never believed in anything. My father had left us, and in the aftermath, my mother became a drunk. She allowed her alcoholism to escalate to the point of an alcohol-induced form of dementia. Despite this, she still had her good days.

On one particular day, she told me that as we die we remember every good thing that has ever happened to us, and the big stuff that changed our lives to make us the person we would become in death. For once, I could say she was right.

I was remembering everything backward. I remembered the last moment I shared with my brother, with Everett, with Mackynsie. I remembered everything I thought was stored in my memory box that used to be my brain. Then it started going farther back. I could see a man picking me up and spinning me around.

"Faster, Daddy! Faster!" I shouted. I didn't think this was real, based on the fact I never knew my father. The memories slowed enough for me to see every part of them—whereas the ones with Ben, Mackynsie, and Everett were like flashes on the television screen. This was different. It was like I was living in the moment with them.

I could see myself as a toddler, maybe only two or three. My hair was just below my ears, and it was full of bouncy ringlets. Soon after this it was like a movie that was panning out from me and onto the whole scene. I saw Ben playing with his Tonka trucks in the grass, and then a man's hands gripped me tightly, spinning me around.

"Brenna," a deep voice, heavy with a foreign accent said to me. "I don't want you to get sick. You had a lot of cotton candy today."

"More, more!" I shouted.

***

A shock to my deadened heart sent me bursting into a place that was bright with lights. From above, I could see myself lying, intubated, on a surgical table. Someone was shaving my head.

"Come on, beautiful. This is nothing compared to what we've seen. You were brave, and you did something most wouldn't do. Don't die for this." It was a nurse whispering into my ear, and though I tried to move closer to her, I felt like I was tethered down between where I was and where I had been.

"Your friends and your brother tell me you're a fighter. Show me that fight you've got in you. You need all of it if you want to come out of this. Promise me you'll come out of this."

Everything went black again.

I was back where I was before I saw myself with the nurse. I was Brenna again, whoever she was, and I was wearing a pink ruffled dress along with a tiara.

"H-h-happy b-b-birthday, s-s-sis—siss-a!" Ben stuttered with a slight lisp. I never knew Ben had speech impediments as a child. There was my mother, and I wondered why she looked so happy. I had never seen my mother happy. The man from earlier came over. He was pale as snow, and he had raven black hair, much like mine. He placed a small chocolate cake on the edge of my high chair, and it had a little candle in the shape of the number one. It was my first birthday. I never saw pictures of this— though, I had seen pictures of me in that very dress with Ben.

"Make a wish, Brenna," the man whispered to me. He got behind me, and that's when I saw our likeness. I had his viridian green eyes, the same black hair, and even a similar facial structure. His cheeks were slightly flushed like mine, except they weren't nearly as rosy. I smashed my hand down into the cake, and the man laughed with pure joy.

"Brennan! Don't let her make a mess! That dress was expensive," my mother shrieked.

Apparently she was still the same even before she began to drink: brash and critical. Ben joined me in the chocolate mess that I had created, and Brennan, the man that looked so much like me, took pictures.

***

177

I felt the shock to my heart again, and a warmth took over me as I traveled from my bank of memories to where my body lay on the table. My head had been wrapped with gauze, and I was hooked up to an IV, along with many cords and lines. I still had a tube down my throat, and when it whirred, my chest puffed up then went down. It was helping me breathe. I looked around and noticed all of the other dying people. Was this where we waited to meet our maker? When I looked up, I saw Ben sitting at my side with a man in a white lab coat next to him, placing his hand on my brother's shoulder.

"These next few hours are critical. If she makes it through the night, it'll be good. If she wakes up, we'll know more. The bullet penetrated her brain in the side that affects memory and speech. Until she wakes up, if she wakes up, we won't know if there was any real damage. Brain surgery is tough on one's mind and soul as well, so we never know how they will be when they wake up."

Ben was sniffling and holding my hand as he listened to the doctor.

"If I were you, I'd let her friends say a few words to her. It can help you and her."

His words were trying to convey something other than what he was saying. He was saying that my friends should say goodbye in case I died in the morning. They should say their final goodbyes, just in case. The doctor left the room, leaving my brother alone in his sadness. I wanted nothing more than to be there and comfort him, and I was unable. I couldn't hear what he was saying as I was being pulled back to the bank of memories.

The next thing I saw was my brother and me on a beach. He was teaching me to build a sand castle, but I was more interested in digging a hole in the sand. I kept hearing the click of a disposable camera.

"D-D-Daddy, s-s-top t-taking p-p-pictchas!" Ben stuttered.

The man he called "Daddy" giggled, and I saw myself stomp over to Ben and point toward the whole with my shovel.

"In," I said.

"F-f-fine." Ben got in and let me bury him with sand. I laughed with a happy lilt, and I sat next to him and put the shovel in my lap. I heard the clicking again and remembered a picture I had seen of this exact moment.

"I love you two with all of my heart," Daddy said, and his voice sounded as if he was crying behind his words.

***

The invisible tether loosened on me, and I went back to the real world where the grown up Ben sat at my bedside, holding my hand. I swore I could feel his hands' warmth against mine.

"There's a lot I never got to tell you, Frances. I can't bear to do it now. If you don't have the fight in you, though, I'll understand. If you don't have the fight, I suppose I won't need to explain much. If there's a heaven, that's where you'll go, and someone will be waiting for you there. He will tell you everything I never could." Ben swiped away the tears and wiped his nose with a tissue. "I'm going to let the guys come see you, and then we've got to wait outside. You need all the rest you can get. I love you, kid." He kissed to my hand and brushed my hair out of my face then got up to leave.

Everything fast-forwarded itself then. Grayson came in. He was showing me pictures of his fiancé and his daughter. He told me he loved me the way he loved his little girl. I wanted to cry—although, nothing came out.

After Grayson told me how proud of me he was and how brave I was, he imparted some last-minute advice to me.

"You are such a bright light, Bea. It'd be a shame to see it go out like this. Don't stop shining. The world hasn't seen nearly enough of you yet, and you haven't seen enough of the world. I know you are a fighter, and I understand if it's too much, but..." He choked up. "...please fight like you would any other day. Promise me you'll try. I want you to meet my daughter, and I want you to be at my wedding. I want to see you grow older and make good and bad decisions. Please stay." He squeezed my hand and left.

After he left, Rian came in. He paced back and forth, whispering to himself, then sat down next to me and held my hand gingerly in his. He was trembling, and the look in his eyes made me know that this wasn't something easy for him. He didn't speak to me, and I could tell that he didn't have enough words to express his feelings.

"Don't stop living, Bea. Just...don't."

After a while, Splinter came in, and he had a guitar in his hands. I didn't know how good of a guitar player he was, so I wasn't sure if I was in for a treat or my entrance musical number for my trip to Hell. As he sat down, he said, "I'm sorry if I do an injustice by playing this to you during a time like this, but I feel I need to do this, so I'm sorry if it isn't very good." He strummed the guitar to check the tuning and started playing one of my songs. He sang the words I had yet to sing—it was exactly as it was in my head. The little shit had been spying in my song journals.

"Nothing ever hurt as much as this,
as much as this—as much as this.
Nothing ever hurt as much as losing you.
All these scars are from when I saw you fall for me.
These scars are from when you lost your light for
me.
It's my fault, and nothing ever hurt,
as much as this, as much as this. "

When he was done playing, he propped the guitar up against the side table with the utmost care, and then he grabbed my hand, cradling it in his two warm hands.

"Bea—Frances, whatever the hell your name is...I know you're probably going to hate me when you come out of this, if you come out of this, and found out I was putting your songs together for you." He shook his head, squeezed my hand tightly. "Screw it; I know you better than you think, Bea.

You are a fighter. That doctor underestimates your annoying stubbornness. He underestimates the love around you and how it fuels you." He paused and sucked in a deep breath. "I hate that you can do this to me. You barely know me, you barely like me on a good day, you could be dying right now, and I'm crying over of it. You're so cold, and yet you're still filled with a sort of warmth I can't un-see. I don't want this to be my last memory of you. I understand why you felt so different after losing Everett. Just a little. It's not a competition, but I think I've got a worse hand than you did then." He laughed bitterly. He was wearing his hair in a loose bun, and pieces of hair fell to frame his face.

"Bea, I can't lose you. I finally got to know you. Like, really know you. You're so compassionate. You chose to die for your own brother when he was so willing to die for you. Who does that? I don't know...I suppose that answers one question. Bea, you shine so bright it's blinding on a good day. I don't want to see you fade away like a shooting star. You're not so fleeting, so don't start that shit now. You need to do a lot still; there's so much unfinished business for you. You need to go to Dartmouth and write music. You need to be the first in your family to go to college and finish.

"You need to make music, like really make it. Whether someone else's voice is singing the lyrics or not, you need to spread your words out into the world. You need to fall in love with the right person. I don't know who that'll be for you— though, I would hope you live long enough to find them. You need to have children. I know not every woman wants children, and I don't know if you're one of them except I can't help but imagine you with a daughter who raises as much Hell as you do on of your good days. I want you to relive your childhood through a mother's eyes. I want you to have amazing experiences, I want you to travel and see every corner of this place we call earth."

Splinter trembled harder, and I realized he was ready to say what he had been intending to say all along.

"Bea, I want you to live. If not for the things I want you to do, then do it for your brother and those guys that are like your family. I never thought anything could separate them, but you are the glue that kept them together. You need to live...they need you too. So don't pussy out now—you've got a lot to do still, and someone has to watch out for those guys. Someone has to help Ben with his hair. Can you believe...never mind." He was crying in earnest now, and he kissed my forehead gently. I felt it, and it brought warmth all over me.

"Just live, dammit. You need to." He squeezed my hands and let go, wiping his tears and forcing himself to leave.

I could feel myself spinning in a room that wasn't quite moving. Every memory, every ounce of love filled me from the bottom of my feet to the top of my head. It filled me until there was no more room, and soon enough, there was a bright, blinding light and another shock to my heart. I went back to the memories, and I saw one I couldn't believe. I saw a tombstone that read:

Brennan Morrison
Loving Son, Husband
and Father

Suddenly we were back in the place I had seen what little memories of Brennan I had. I was in my mother's lap, and Ben's face was red and puffy from crying. He was wearing black, and so was our mother. Even the two-year-old me was wearing a black dress.

"Mommy, why do you keep calling Brenna—?"

My mother harshly interrupted a stutter-less Ben from his question. "Her name is no longer Brenna, Ben. We're going to call her Frances."

I was looking at my birth certificates—plural. One that appeared to be the original had the name Brenna Seirian Rose Morrison on it with the father listed as Brennan Morrison. The other one, that appeared to be newer, had the name I knew now— Frances Beatrice Morrison. There was no father listed.

Ben looked confused. "Why, Mommy?"

"We need to forget your father," she said simply. "Your father is gone. Frances won't ever remember him, and it'll be best for all of us to pretend he was never here. So when she asks, we will tell her he ran off before she was born."

Hot tears stung my eyes, and burned a trail down my face.

"Now take your sister to your room. Mommy needs an adult drink."

She dropped me from her lap, and the two-year-old me cried loudly as ten-year-old Ben took me to his room. Our mother opened up a bottle of her favorite liquor, and it all began to make sense.

My life was a lie. This whole time our mother had raised Ben and me to pretend that we never had a loving father. My heart was racing, and slowly but surely, I could feel it pounding in my chest. I was getting my fight back. Right then, I remembered all the horrible things. I remembered every night I went to sleep with tears in my eyes and anger in my heart belonging to a father who had no idea of who I was and who had left me with the mother who did nothing but drink herself sick.

I remembered all the nights Ben held me while I cried in fear as mother trashed our apartment or made us move in the middle of the night. I remembered all the things that followed, and most of all, I remembered him: Brennan. I remembered all the times I had been called Brenna and thought my mother was delusional, and I remembered all the nights she called out his name. His face popped in and out of this vision or that dream or whatever it was. I felt furious and filled with passion all at once.

I have to live.

"I *have* to live," I said aloud. "I HAVE TO *LIVE!*"

Everything rushed into me. There was life and love, anger and sadness, and even joy and contentment. Everything rushed through me, and it didn't feel like very long—though when I returned to my hospital room, I was being taken off the ventilator. Though I struggled at first to breathe on my own, my lungs started working.

Whatever my physical self was unable to do, I was unable to do in this in-between state of self. I focused on my brother and all the times he had to have wanted to tell me the truth only to lie to protect me from the hurt. I thought of all the times I had been hurt and he'd gone out of his way to protect me. I thought of every single thing he had ever done for me just from the fact that I was his baby sister, and I felt a pang in my chest.

Fading into the darkness again, I wasn't sure where I was—though, I knew that I was traveling toward something. As I got closer I got to it, I saw it was a light much like the light at the end of a tunnel. I was determined to live, and I was going to make damned sure that I would never go through this again.

I thought of Everett and his love for me, and I thought of Mackynsie and our sisterhood that would live on despite her absence. I thought of my father, the man I never really knew that I knew. I thought of how he loved me. I thought of my brother, and of all the memories we had shared together, all the memories we had made this summer.

I wasn't ready for it to end.

The light was getting brighter, and I was feeling warmer by the second. Senses and sensations were coming back to me; the light was shining brighter than ever, and it was expanding.

This is it, I thought.

This was the moment of truth. Whether I lived or I died, this was it. The light grew wider and ever more blinding until it swallowed me up, and then there was nothing.

I could still hear the beeping of machines and the sound of crying nearby. I felt a hand on mine...eyelashes resting on my cheek and my heart beating slowly. I thought about my toes wiggling.

They moved!

I tried to squeeze my hands, and my grip tightened around the person holding my hand, who shouted for the doctors.

"It's just a reflex," one nurse said.

My eyelids fluttered, and I tried to open my eyes. My viridian green eyes with the sectoral heterochromia underneath my left iris opened, my pale cheeks flushing with color. All I could see was the ceiling above me. The lights were too bright. I blinked a couple of times to adjust, and someone shouted for Ben and for a doctor nearby. Even the nurse was paging the doctor hurriedly. No one expected me to be awake.

The doctor was flashing his little light in my eyes, and I did the silly commands he asked me to do. Follow his light, grip his fingers, and wiggle my toes.

"What's your name?" he asked.

"Frances," I croaked out.

"How old are you?"

"Eighteen," I said with a clearer voice.

"Do you know what happened to you?"

My mind went blank.

"Frances, you were shot in the head trying to save your brother. You're safe now." He patted my hands and went to talk to Ben.

I tried to let everything sink into me. I was alive.

187

I had been shot, and I survived. My brother killed a man to save both me and himself.

Everything was slowly coming back to me. Ben sat down and held my hand, laying his head in my lap and sobbing with relief. I let go of his hand and ran mine through his hair in a motherly fashion.

"I made you a promise," I said. My voice was still slightly hoarse—though, I could feel it getting better. A nurse came by and gave me a cup of water, and I drank it slowly while I gave my brother time to process.

"Frances, I can't bear to lose you again."

I didn't know what he meant by that, yet I looked to him and smiled weakly.

"I made you a promise, Ben. A silent one, but a promise nonetheless."

He looked up at me in confusion. "What are you saying, Frances?"

"I promised I'd always be in your heart, and you promised me the same. You promised you'd keep the faith, and you did—because I'm okay." It was my turn to let the tears flow, and when they started, I couldn't stop.

I cried for hours with my brother by my side, and when I was ready, I looked up to him.

"You said you had a lot to tell me still," I told him. "Well, I think I know most of it."

He looked at me with astonishment, and I laughed.

"I could hear you when you talked to me. When I wasn't hearing you, I was remembering things on my own."

"What did you remember, Frances?"

I sighed heavily and wiped my face with the cheap hospital-issued tissue paper.

"I remembered everything, Ben."

He looked at me with more fear in his eyes than I had ever seen.

"Frances—"

"Don't call me that."

"Why not? It's your name."

I never had a chance to respond. Soon enough, doctors flooded the room as did our friends. It was a time for celebration on behalf of my miraculous recovery. The doctors told me there would be more to living now that I had a brain injury even if it was minor. I had to wait and hope that Ben would loosen his grip on the lie I knew he was telling. No matter what it was that I had experienced, I knew something, and that something was that I had no idea who I really was anymore.

EPILOUGE

After a day full of celebration and appointment-making, phone calls, and final arrangements, I was moved to a private room, and I finally got Ben to myself. He was sitting quietly in the far corner, avoiding my gaze. We both knew what was going to be our next topic of conversation. I wanted him to bring it up though it was obvious he would rather I give the first fatal blow.

"Ben?"

He looked up as if he had been sleeping. He was distraught, and he didn't know what to expect next.

"Yes, Bea?"

"Please don't call me that."

"What do you want to be called?"

I didn't know what I wanted to be called. I didn't know my options anymore. My entire life it was Frances or Bea, but never Beatrice. Now I had to cut straight to the chase and figure out what truth my near-death experience had to the life I've lead. I took a deep breath and readied myself for the emotional conversation for which we were long overdue.

"I think it's time we talk about our dad, Ben."

He looked confused and worried all at once. I didn't want to look at him after that. It was too hard to watch his emotions spread across his face.

"Why do you want to talk about him?" he asked.

"He never left us, did he?"

His eyes widened with the obvious fear of my newfound knowledge.

"He never left, not in the way I had been told, did he, Ben?"

"Bea, there's a lot that has happened…maybe you're confused."

"I am *not* confused!"

I knew he was lying. It showed across his face. There was guilt, and there was sadness and remorse.

"Tell me the truth, Ben. The real truth."

He shook his head. "I can't do it, Frances. I don't want to lose you."

"You keep saying that, and I don't know why. Please tell me something to help me understand." I was begging now, tears streaming down my face. "Ben, I saw things. I don't know if it was the in-between or limbo or what, but I saw things. I won't know how true they are or if they are real memories until you tell me the truth. The whole truth."

"Brenna, don't do this to—"

He said exactly what I had needed him to. I'd caught him in the middle of a sixteen-year-old lie.

"Who is Brenna?"

Ben stood abruptly, knocking his chair loudly to the tiled floor.

"Tell me the truth, Ben!" I shouted.

"I'm not doing this! I'm in too deep—it's too

late to change anything." He was pacing back and forth, running his hands up and down his face and through his hair. He was a mess.

"Change what?"

"You want the truth? I lied. Mom lied. We lied together. We had a father, and he loved us. You especially," he laughed bitterly. "You were the most perfect daughter he could ever want. When you were born, you were all he wanted. It was as if I didn't exist anymore."

"What happened to him?"

Ben kicked the chair back up and sat down in it, spreading his legs and propping his elbows up on his knees. "He died." He laughed again. "Our parents were living in separate places. They shared us like we shared toys. He was dropping us off from the beach, and you didn't want him to leave."

As he was saying this, I could see it in my head. I remember the same bathing suit I saw in the memory from the in-between and from the photographs I found of Ben and me together when I was cleaning out my room.

"You ran out into the street, and a driver was coming through over the speed limit."

My mouth hung open, and I covered it with my hand. I could remember it now. It was coming back. It was another lightning bolt, and it tore right through me.

"Our father, Brennan, he loved you so much he named you after him. He pushed you out of the way and was hit by the car himself. It was a fatal crash. The car ran straight over him, and he didn't survive the hit-and-run."

Breathing erratically, I was crying horribly with what felt like little screams trying to come out of my throat.

"Why did you lie, Ben? Why did you—?"

"Because Mother was in love with him despite all the crap even though she was crazy. If she couldn't have him, neither could we. She began drinking more than her daily sacrament wine, she changed your name, and all due to the fact that it reminded her of him too much. The alcohol was the only thing to fill the hole in her heart, and your name had more of him than anything else."

I didn't really know who I was anymore. Who was Brenna? She was just a girl in pictures I always assumed was named Bea. But who was Bea? She had changed so much in such a short time—it was hard to tell who was really who. What made them different? What made them the same? *Were* they different? *Were* they the same?

"Who am I, Ben?" I asked tearfully.

"You were born Brenna Seirian Rose Morrison. Mother changed your name to Frances Beatrice Morrison the week of our father's funeral."

"But, Ben, who *am* I?"

"I just told you—"

"I know the names I've been given. *Who am I?* Am I Frances, or am I Brenna?"

"I don't know. That's all up to you now. Who do you think you are?"

I had to really think, and the more I thought, the more lost I was. As far as I was concerned, I was no one. Maybe I wasn't anyone at all.

Ben had to leave when visiting hours were over,

and now, my room was silent. There would be no real answer to my question anytime soon. I knew I could try and persuade him to give me the answers about Brennan, our father, that I wanted—though as days passed and he would come visit, I found it was too much to bear. Ben and I argued so often for so long, and some days, I'd forget entirely what we had been arguing about until Splinter mentioned it to me.

"So this is it then. You won't tell me a single thing?" I asked him.

"Not right now, Bea."

"Please don't call me that."

"It's your name!"

"And apparently so is Brenna!"

Silence came over us, and he sighed.

"Look, I need to head to New Hampshire to make sure everything is in order. You'll be alone for a week, but I'm sure you'll be fine.

"Maybe you'll be able to let this go in that time. I'll see you when you get back." He pressed a kiss to my head, and once he left and the nurse returned, she asked me a question.

"Are you sure you've made your mind?" Looking to her, I nodded

"Yes, I don't want any visitors. Not my brother, not my friends or his bandmates, no one."

"You'll do much better if you—"

"I know what I'm doing. Please just give me the proper paperwork so we can get this over with."

When Ben came back the next week, he was surprised to find out I asked for no visitors. He came back every day, and every day, he became angrier and more demanding. He only wanted to see me, and I refused to see him. I can't remember when he stopped coming, but I knew I had to do this by myself. If he couldn't tell me who I was; I needed to figure it out for myself...even if that meant reopening every single scar until it bled the truth for me. Because the exit wound that was left behind from this summer was one I'd never forget, and I needed to gain every ounce of strength I had in order to fight the demons that were living inside my head. I wasn't going to lose this fight; I needed a reason to fight back, and through all the rehab and physical therapy, I discovered the reason to fight back was so I could prove that I was not in ruins. I know what can be done to destroy a city, to destroy a populous or even a single person, and now I knew the warning signs of someone who was out to destroy me. I wouldn't let it happen again.

With camera people coming in and out constantly and social media outlets questioning everything about who I was and what I was doing, I needed to be prepared. I couldn't back out of the spotlight anymore; I was no longer my brother's secret. I was open, naked, and vulnerable to the whole world.

I refused to let them see me that way. I fought, and I fought until I thought I had dealt with everything. Then I'd wake up from seeing Everett's bloody shirt or Mackynsie's mangled face, and I'd do it all over again. It wasn't a matter of doing it just to get better anymore. It was a matter of doing it so I could look back and say I survived even if it didn't matter anymore. This wasn't my ending. I was determined to get my life back. This was only the prologue.

ACKNOWLEDGMENTS

I'd like to thank the following people for their contribution into making this book, my life's work and dream, become a possibility.

Cary L. Schultz Stanley, my wise beyond her years best friend and soul sister: thank you for always listening to me rant about this book, day or night, finals or no finals, lots of homework or no homework, bad day or good day. Thank you for putting up with me for so long, and thank you for inspiring me to be a better person and to forgive more often.

Megan Jackson, the most amazing CP and Beta-Reader I could have ever come across in my life. You helped me day and night with this story, and you fell in love with it just as I did so many years ago. Thank you for being patient with me, and for dedicating all of your free time to editing this novel for me. When this is in print, I owe you another coffee date.

To my Local Library and Writing Group: Thanks for being excited with me when I finished this novel, for telling me how good it was, and for celebrating with me when I told y'all I got this publishing deal. I am so grateful for you ladies and gents. I hope I'll be able to be a good writing group manager always.

Mom, Dad, Munner, Grandpa: Thank you for putting up with me for twenty-one years, Mom. Thanks for choosing me, Dad. Thanks for putting up with the late night paper jams, low-ink beeping and printer hogging, Munner. And Grandpa, thanks for taking all my crap, and promptly ignoring it. I love you all, even though you do really drive me mad.

And finally, to Kristopher R. Benitez: My best friend, and love of my life. I'm glad I can call you both. Thank you for always putting up with my craziness, and for just rolling with the punches. Thank you for all the times you've spent just listening to me rant about this book while I was writing, editing, revising, or doing anything remotely work-like with it. Thank you for giving me the chance to share this experience with you. Because that is something I want to be able to do the rest of our lives. So prepare to become bored and annoyed with me as I embark on making more stories, because you're going to hear about it a lot more very soon.

ABOUT THE AUTHOR

My name is Alexandra Moore. I've been creating stories since I could talk. I've been putting them onto paper since I could write. Writing books is my dream and my passion, along side with rescuing African Pygmy Hedgehogs, retired race Greyhounds, French Bulldogs, and other various animals I'm probably allergic too.

I'm convinced I'm the blood of the dragon, and the Mother of Dragons.

When I'm not watching GoT, I'm watching Grey's Anatomy (again) on Netflix, and crying over all the MerDer feels. I also spend time with my Boston Terrier Tank and my boyfriend. Both are my cuddle buddies, and I'm afraid the dog is around more often. I don't bite (unless provoked) so feel free to tweet at me, or leave a comment on one of my InstaPics. I can't wait until my book is in print, and to share my thoughts with the rest of the world.

Facebook:
https://www.facebook.com/authoralexandramoore

Twitter:
https://twitter.com/amooreauthor

Instagram:
https://instagram.com/a.m.author

51019467R00124

Made in the USA
Charleston, SC
09 January 2016